A Golden Web

BARBARA QUICK

HARPER TEEN

An Imprint of HarperCollinsPublishers

For my extraordinary son—
needless to say, with love

HarperTeen is an imprint of HarperCollins Publishers.

A Golden Web
Copyright © 2010 by Barbara Quick
All rights reserved. Printed in the United States of America.
No part of this book may be used or reproduced in any manner whatsoever without
written permission except in the case of brief quotations embodied in critical articles
and reviews. For information address HarperCollins Children's Books, a division
of HarperCollins Publishers, 10 East 53rd Street, New York, NY 10022.
www.harperteen.com

Library of Congress Cataloging-in-Publication Data
Quick, Barbara.
  A golden web / Barbara Quick. — 1st ed.
    p. cm.
  Summary: In fourteenth-century Bologna, Alessandra Giliani, a brilliant young
girl, defies convention and risks death in order to attend medical school at the
university so that she can study anatomy.
  ISBN 978-0-06-144887-4 (trade bdg.)
  1. Giliani, Alessandra, 1307-1326—Juvenile fiction. [1. Giliani, Alessandra,
1307-1326—Fiction. 2. Sex role—Fiction. 3. Anatomy—Fiction. 4. Bologna
(Italy)—History—Middle Ages, 600-1500—Fiction. 5. Italy—History—1268-
1492—Fiction.] I. Title.
PZ7.Q3183Go 2010   2009014265
[Fic]—dc22   CIP
                                                                    AC

Typography by Joel Tippie

10 11 12 13 14   CG/RRDB   10 9 8 7 6 5 4 3 2 1
❖
First Edition

Prologue

A beautiful baby lay in her cradle, watched over by a nanny still nursing the infant's rosy big brother. The wet-nurse, both famous and feared for her knowledge of plants and nostrums, had placed a bowl of water beneath the cradle. Into this bowl she dropped three oak apples, plucked at break of dawn from the crooked branches of an ancient tree that grew outside the nursery window.

The baby had, the night before, looked up from the nanny's breast, smacked her lips, and said, as clear as day, *"Delizioso!"*

If the oak apples sank instead of floating, the nanny would know for certain that this child—with such an unnaturally bright look in its eyes—was a changeling, put in the cradle by a devil who had snatched the real baby away with him at a moment when the nurse's attention was somewhere else.

She had her knife at the ready. She was watching the oak apples with such intensity—one hand on the good boy baby and the other on the knife—that she neither saw nor heard her mistress come into the room.

With the strength and swiftness born of her love, Signora Giliani wrested both the knife and her son out of the nurse's grasp and snatched her baby daughter out of the cradle. The bowl of water, stained brown by the oak apples, spilled out over the flagstones.

"Leave this house!" she said, her voice raked by the horror of what had nearly happened.

The nanny looked not at her mistress but at the bright-eyed infant, who was watching everything unfold with a look of intelligence the nurse had never seen before, in all the babes she'd ever suckled. A word—and not just any word, but such a fancy word—at eight months old!

Signora Giliani spoke again. "Leave now, and God help you if I ever see you anywhere near my children!"

When the woman was gone and the young mother had stilled her heart, she allowed her winsome boy to stand by her while she unwrapped the infant and made sure she hadn't been harmed. She kissed the baby's silken shoulders, breathed in the good scent of her, then wrapped her up again, holding her safe and close.

"Alessandra, my angel!" she half whispered, half sang. Then she bent down and kissed her firstborn's blond hair. "Nicco," she said, looking into his blue eyes that were so like his father's. "You will help us watch over your baby sister, won't you?"

The baby heard her mother's voice accompanied by the comforting sound of her mother's heart—and she knew, though only an infant, that she was loved. She thought the word again that she'd said before—*"Delizioso!"*—one of the several words she'd come to associate with feelings or things. Her world was a bright and shining place, so filled with wonders that she was loath to ever close her eyes to it.

"If anything should happen to me, Nicco," Alessandra heard her mother murmur, although she couldn't understand yet what the words meant, nor the grief they portended, "you must stand by her always."

One

Nicco was scared. His tutor was going to burst through the door at any moment, and Alessandra was nowhere to be found. Not in her room, not in the library, not in the chicken coop watching the damn chickens—who but his ridiculous little sister could spend hours watching chickens? Not in the barn, not in the kitchen, not in their tree house, not in the nursery. And today, of all days, when he was going to be grilled on Aristotle!

He eyed the window, fitted with the waxed linen screen—the only one of its kind in Persiceto, imported all the way from Rome and such a source of pride to his stepmother. She'd smacked him hard, more than once, for falling against it or touching it with sticky fingers. He could just pull it open on its clever hinge, if he dared. In two minutes flat, he'd be across the courtyard and onto the towpath. If he was lucky, he could catch a barge all the way to Bologna.

The entryway door clanged shut. *Oh, please, sweet Jesus,* Nicco prayed, *let Emilia offer the blighter a nip of brandy!* Dear Emilia, watching over each of them in turn since Alessandra was a baby, usually carried a little flask of spirits—for emergencies, she always told the children— tucked into her bodice.

Nicco ran his fingers up and down the page he was supposed to have mastered, wishing he could coax or comb the words into some order that would make more sense to him. What a blasted son of a monkey that Aristotle was, no doubt having made it his life's purpose to trip up brave and honest boys in the sleep-inducing twists and turns of his prose!

There was the sound of giggling outside the door. *That's it, Emilia—reach for the flask and give him an eyeful of*

your flesh! Just buy me a little time! What does it matter if he looks?
Your bosom is as goodly a thing to look upon as any cathedral.

With a sinking heart, Nicco heard the sound of a slap. *Oh, God, Emilia—how could you? That slap of yours will transform itself into a beating for me faster than my dog gets fleas!* Nicco scratched at a bite beneath his jerkin, then swore, cutting off the oath just in time for it to turn into a greeting for his fat, flustered, and now red-faced tutor.

"Fra Giuseppe!" said Nicco, bowing low and wincing in anticipation of his tutor's customary greeting—a blow with his stick across Nicco's buttocks, if he was lucky, rather than on his face or hands. "For the errors you are about to make," Fra Giuseppe would say in Latin, as if this qualified the action as part of Nicco's education.

Nicco raised his face when no blow came, and looked with a sudden rush of hope and gratitude into the bloodshot blue eyes of the friar, who always smelled of mice and drink.

Fra Giuseppe waited until Nicco was upright and then caught him with a snap of the stick at the backs of his knees, making them buckle. "Stop staring, you blockhead! Thinking of escaping, were you?"

How did he know? Nicco got to his feet, careful to keep his eyes trained on the floor. He prayed to St. Anthony to come to his rescue, but then stopped himself short when he realized what a sin it would be to call for the sudden death of a priest, if only such a one as Fra Giuseppe, in minor orders and known as one of the most energetic sinners in the parish. Would it be a sin to pray for the friar to be struck with palsy, so that he would be unable to wield that stick of his? Or to come over paralyzed all of a sudden, just like the swineherd, Tommaso, who was found in the piazza just two days past, alive but as stiff as a plank, unable to move even so much as a finger?

"Aristotle," came the tutor's grating voice. He bent his face close to Nicco's, so close that Nicco held his breath, willing the priest away from his nostrils before he was forced to inhale. "It's a newly cut stick, my boy. Not yet broken in."

Nicco had thought it felt less pliant than the old one— the backs of his knees were still stinging. What a plague all teachers were! How could Alessandra possibly long for their company with the same ardor Nicco felt for the horse his father had given him to mark his fourteenth year?

And no sooner did Nicco think of his sister than she appeared in the doorway, a curly-haired shrimp of a girl with her green velvet gown all spattered in mud.

"Fra Giuseppe," she said, eyes downcast and curtsying just like a proper lady. "Emilia has requested your help with a knotty spiritual question, Padre. She is waiting for you in the hut behind the rose garden."

A tender smile floated across the friar's face. "Ah, yes, I certainly must go to her. You!" he said to Nicco.

"Yes, sir."

"I will question you when I return. Um—"

"Yes, Padre?"

"If your dear mother comes to check upon our lessons . . ."

"We will be sure to tell her, Padre, that you were called away on an urgent spiritual matter," said Alessandra, dropping another curtsy. Nicco thought she was laying it on a bit thick.

But the friar only licked his lips as if he'd just tasted something wonderful. "Yes, an urgent spiritual matter."

He turned to Nicco again. "What a shame, blockhead, that you do not have even a finger's-breadth of the mental agility of this mere girl!" Then he was out the door with the swiftness of an arrow.

"Well done, dear Sis!"

"For the moment, perhaps. But he's going to be piping mad when he gets to the hut and finds no one there but the gardener, who's already in a horrible mood because I trampled his turnips, quite by accident, while trying to catch the new piglet that had wandered off—and now I've ruined my gown, and Mother is surely going to kill me."

"Don't call her Mother, not to my face." Nicco noticed a purpling bruise on the back of his sister's hand. "Has she struck you again?"

Alessandra did her best to hide her hand in the folds of her sleeve. "She makes me call her Mother."

"Well, she shouldn't, God knows, the way she treats you!"

Alessandra leaned up close to her brother, taking in the good smell of the outdoors that always clung to his clothes. "She's not as bad as some."

"She is going to kill you when she sees the wreck

you've made of your gown!" said Nicco as he pushed her gently away. "Isn't that the one Father brought back for you from Firenze?"

"It was the piglet, Nic—he was terribly slippery, and the turnips had just been set out in their rows."

Nicco tousled his sister's hair. "You're as hopeless a well-behaved girl as I am a scholar. Which reminds me . . . !"

Alessandra turned away from him to examine the book that stood open on its stand. "Oh, I parsed this out last harvest season. Look, let's just go over it so that you can at least do a passable job when he comes back, and I'll see if I can find an excuse to stay close by, so that I can help you out with a whispered answer, if need be. Did you know that he's deaf in the left ear?"

"I had no idea, you witch! How do you know these things?"

"I pay attention, sausage-head. Now, you do the same—and hurry up, because he'll be coming through the door again before the noontime bells are rung. If we're lucky, he really will find Emilia, and she'll be nice to him after that lordly slap she just gave him."

"I thought you were in the pigsty!"

"One hears these things if one stays alert, Nicco. Come on, now. '*Aequiuoca dicuntur quorum nomen solum commune est . . .*'" Alessandra muttered the rest of the Latin phrase. "This works out to something like 'Things are said to be named "equivocally" when, although they have the same name, they're actually different things.' It's a way of talking about the relationship between the language we use to describe things and the things themselves."

Nicco looked at her blankly. "What difference does it make what I call a thing?"

"Okay, think of it this way. Mother and our stepmother are both, in our language, *una donna*—a woman. But you and I know there's a world of difference between them, even though the same word is used to describe them both."

An expression of understanding dawned on Nicco's face. "Bloody hell, Alessandra, you're too clever by half!"

Two

They were not ten minutes into parsing out the passage from Aristotle when Domenico, caged inside his baby walker, bumped up against the half-open door.

Alessandra managed to catch her youngest sibling mid-fall. "Dodo, my little love! What are you doing out of the nursery?"

The two-year-old was all smiles at the success of the journey he'd taken on his own. He threw his sturdy little arms around his sister's neck, crowing his own version of her name: "Zan-Zan!"

"He doesn't even have his booties on," said Nicco. "Madame our stepmother will be livid if she finds out he's wandered off on his own again. Was it you or Emilia supposed to be watching him?"

"Emilia—but never mind. Look how tall he's getting, Nicco! I think babies must grow in the nighttime—he already needs a new band sewn to the bottom of his gown."

Alessandra gathered Dodo into her arms, smoothing the feathery tufts of his blond hair. "Doesn't he look like an angel? We must get Old Fabio to paint an image of him in the new book he's working on."

"Old Fabio seems much more inclined to use devils than angels in his decorations these days."

Just then, Emilia herself, rosier than usual and spattered in what looked distinctly like blood, appeared in the doorway, wringing her hands. "I am undone!" she wailed.

"Why, Emilia," said Alessandra, handing off the baby to Nicco, "what's happened?"

Emilia, a full head taller than twelve-year-old Alessandra, and twice as wide, nevertheless managed to collapse into the child's arms. "It's the friar," she sobbed into the chestnut-brown curls. "I gave him a piece of meat and a bowl of wine, feeling rather badly at the way I'd handled him earlier. And he no sooner had a sup of it than he clawed at the air and came over all possessed, barking and snorting like Satan himself!"

"Oh, God," groaned Nicco, "it is my doing!"

"Hush, Nic! And then what happened?"

"Why, the Devil must have grabbed him by the hair, for he fell straight backwards!" Emilia wept harder. "And there he lay, his eyes rolled back and the earth just beneath him shaking so hard, I thought it would open up and swallow him!"

Alessandra looked accusingly at her brother. "Did you poison the wine, Nic? You could have killed us all!"

"I didn't touch the wine!" Nicco struck his forehead with his fists. "I wished Fra Giuseppe dead today. I prayed to St. Anthony to strike him dead. But I took it back—I swear!"

Dodo began to cry.

"Are you sure he's quite dead, Emilia?" said Alessandra.

Emilia looked up, wiping her nose with the back of

her hand. "I never thought to doubt it. He fell like an oak, and there was blood everywhere."

Alessandra used the hem of her gown to blot Emilia's tears. "'By doubting we come to inquire, and by inquiring we perceive the truth.'"

"Oh, do shut up, Alessandra! Emilia, for the love of God, take us to the old sinner before the Devil claims him!"

They ran then, all three of them—with Dodo perched on his brother's shoulders—outside the house and across the grounds, chickens scattering before them.

Fra Giuseppe's body was sprawled on the raised and fenced platform of flagstones—safe from wolves—where one could overlook the garden. A circlet of blood spread out beneath his head, looking uncannily like a halo. The expression on his face, though, suggested a vision of unspeakable horrors.

"What ill luck," wailed Emilia, "to die without the chance to make his peace with God!"

"It would have taken this one a month to confess all his sins," said Nicco, nudging the friar's body with the toe of his boot. "He's as dead as a pike, God save me!"

Alessandra bent down, close enough to stare into the friar's glassy blue eyes—then farther still, so that her cheek was resting on his chest.

"I know you love learning," said Nicco. "But this is disgusting, Alessandra. He was a loathsome man!"

"Hush!" she said. With her cheek still pressed against the friar's body, she felt along the length of his arm, finding the underside of his wrist and squeezing there.

"Make way, for I'm going to be sick!"

"Oh, do be quiet and help me, Nicco!"

"Help you what? He's dead."

Alessandra stood up and pushed Nicco closer to the body.

"I'll be stuffed before I'll kiss him good-bye!"

"Don't be an idiot! He needs to be stomped on, not kissed. But it has to be just right, and I don't have the strength to do it myself."

"You want me to stomp on the dead friar's body?"

Alessandra knelt down and traced a cross near the top of Fra Giuseppe's belly, between his ribs. "Just here! Stomp on him, hard and sharp, but not hard enough to break his bones."

"And now the child has gone mad!" cried Emilia, crossing herself.

"Please be quiet, both of you! Do what I say, Nic, or he's bound to die!"

"God in Heaven," said Nicco, "this may well be worth a trip to Hell!"

Nicco had expert aim, whether with bow and arrow, his balled fist, or his boot, which no sooner made contact with the place indicated by Alessandra than the priest's jaw dropped open. While Nicco and Emilia both recoiled in horror, Alessandra reached deep inside the friar's foam-flecked mouth and pulled out a half-chewed piece of mutton.

Fra Giuseppe gasped, sputtered, and then cried out in fear when his hands made contact with the pool of his own blood. "Are we attacked?" he said, his voice wobbling.

"You were, dear sir," said Alessandra, tossing the chunk of meat over her shoulder, "but my brother saved you!"

"Alessandra Giliani!" said Emilia, crossing herself again—but Alessandra silenced her by grabbing her hand and giving it an urgent squeeze. A crow flew down from the sky, snatched up the meat, and exultantly flew away with it.

The priest looked up and about him wildly. "Brigands, was it? And in broad daylight! Ouch!" he groaned as he tried to right himself and clutched his ribs. "They've injured me something awful, the villains!" He paused and sniffed the air. "They were mad with drink—they must have been. Who else would be fool enough to try and kill a man of God?"

"Who else indeed?" said Nicco solemnly.

Emilia was about to mutter something else when Alessandra found a handful of flesh through the folds of her nanny's skirts and pinched hard enough to make her cry out instead.

"Do you see them?" asked the friar, looking up at her cry. *"Bastardi!"* he shouted into the distance, shaking his fist.

Alessandra had to cover her mouth to contain her laughter. "Are you wounded, Nic?" she said with tears in her eyes.

Nicco rubbed the backs of his knees where, earlier, the friar had struck him. "Not too badly to run in pursuit of them—if you're sure you're well enough now, Fra Giuseppe."

"Run, dear boy—run like the wind! God will reward you!" His gaze focused then on the upended wine bowl. "I had the oddest dream," he said.

"Run, Nicco!" cried Alessandra, the laughter spilling out of her despite all her best efforts to keep it hidden.

"Like the wind!" said Emilia, daubing at her eyes and shaking.

"Wind!" echoed Dodo as Nicco took off in the direction of the stables to saddle his horse and go for a lovely ride. He would have to work hard, he told himself, to think of a way to repay Alessandra, his excellent Alessandra—who, though only a girl, was smarter and braver than anyone, save their father, in all of Persiceto.

Three

Alessandra caught up with Nicco just as he was tightening Nero's halter. The stallion whinnied at the sight of her, then pushed his huge head against Alessandra's clothes, looking for the windfall apple or pear she usually kept tucked into one of her pockets.

Nicco looked down at his sister with admiration. "What I can't fathom is how you figured out how to bring the old sinner back to life."

"That's an easy one. He was not dead!"

Alessandra held her hand out flat to give Nero his

apple, wary of having her fingers nibbled. "Do you remember that pike you caught, last Whitsuntide—how you stepped on it, just so, and it coughed up the smaller fish it lately swallowed—how the little fish went flying through the air?"

"But a man is not a fish!"

"You made me think of doing the same thing, nonetheless, when you said Fra Giuseppe was 'dead as a pike'—those were your precise words. I already suspected, from what Emilia told us, that some meat might have been caught in his gullet. You know how he gobbles his food!"

Nicco shook his head in wonder. "St. Francis himself might learn a trick or two from you, Sis!"

"You know . . ." Alessandra lowered her voice, even though the two of them were quite alone. "I wouldn't dare say this to anyone else, but I think a good many things that common folks call miracles are merely matters of an observant person's plain good sense."

Nicco climbed up onto his horse. "The miracle will be if you are not burned for a witch before you're grown!"

"Half the trick of being a smart girl is learning how to

hide it." Alessandra stroked Nero's silky muzzle. "Don't look glum, Nic! Fra Giuseppe is bound to give a good report of your progress, now that he fully believes you saved his life. You may even be quit of him as a tutor, as his knowledge doesn't extend much beyond what he's already taught you."

"What he's already taught *you*, it would be fairer to say. It was excessively good of you to give me the credit for saving his life!"

"Goodness had nothing to do with it." Alessandra shivered. "I have no desire to ever serve as fuel for a bonfire in the square."

They were both silent for a moment, remembering the monk who was burned at the stake there the year before—how he'd shouted through the flames that the wrath of God would come down on the sinful puppet who sat on the Pope's throne in Avignon. The smell of burning flesh lingered for days afterwards. "Did you make Emilia promise not to tell?"

"She loves us both too much to ever tell. But, now, Nic, I have a favor to ask of you."

"Ask away! I would be a brute to deny you anything,

after all you've done for me." Nero pawed and snorted, so that Alessandra, straining her neck to look up at them, moved back a couple of paces.

"Teach me to ride, Nic!"

"You have your little pony, and you ride quite prettily already."

"That's not what I mean. I want you to teach me to ride as well as you, and to learn the ways of the woods and all the creatures that live there."

"I will teach you to ride, with pleasure, although you're a bit of a shrimp to handle a horse as big as Nero. But the woods are full of dangers—"

"Which is why I want to learn their ways!" Alessandra looked out to the dark line of trees that marked the beginning of the forest. "I've made a study of all I can, in and around our father's house. I long to go farther afield. You have no idea how galling it is to be penned up here as surely as our cattle."

"Our cattle are penned up to keep them safe from wolves and bears and just the sorts of brigands you convinced Fra Giuseppe had tried to rob him."

"But if you teach me to ride, and read the woods—"

"It is not one of your books!"

"It's one of yours! You've spent your life learning the language of it, just as I've learned Latin. And you will teach me—you must!—just as I've taught you."

"And if something should happen to you?"

Alessandra stood close against Nero's flank and looked up into her brother's blue eyes. "Your knowledge will keep me safe, dear onion—or as safe as a girl with dreams can ever be in this small-minded world."

Alessandra had, for many years now, been in the habit of stealing away with a candle to the storage room. Because there was no window there, and no fire, it was the only room (apart from the privy) where she could usually count on spending time alone.

On each of these visits, she would open the chest that held her mother's wedding dress and everyday clothes. (Her two embroidered gowns and the silk and velvet clothing were all appropriated by her stepmother.) Alessandra would caress the linen and homespun garments that still held a faint scent of the person she'd loved so much and lost. And lately, from the silken folds of the wedding gown, she'd take out the heavy icon of the Virgin, painted by Old Fabio with her mother's likeness. Alessandra held it against her as she prayed, and kissed her mother's face after every whispered *Ave Maria*.

But this day she opened the chest that held the children's own outgrown clothes that could not, as yet, be handed down. Sorting through them until she found some of Nicco's garments that she thought would fit her, she stripped off her gown and kirtle and pulled on breeches and a doublet. With some twisting and tucking, she managed to hide her hair under a cap. She knew the disguise was a good one when her sister walked in on her and let out a mighty shriek.

"Hush, for God's sake, Pierina—it's me!"

"You scared me half to death! I thought we were being robbed. What are you up to, then? I'm sure it can't be any good."

"Mind your own business, pipsqueak! I'm off to study."

"I'm going to tell!"

Alessandra grabbed Pierina by the shoulders and looked into her clear blue eyes, so rare in their part of the world. "Tell what? That I've donned a set of Nicco's castoff clothes?"

"It's some sort of scheme of yours." Pierina wriggled out of her sister's grasp. "Or some game. And I want to play, too! You and Nic always leave me out of everything!"

"We wouldn't if you weren't such a tattletale."

"I won't be this time—I promise! Cross my heart and hope to die!"

"All right, then." Alessandra took Pierina's hand and sat her down on the chest that held their mother's clothes.

Pierina was looking at her expectantly.

"It's a game called Disappearing," said Alessandra.

Pierina nodded sagely.

"I'm to go first, because I'm the elder girl."

"You always get to go first!"

"Hush! The other's job is to cover up while the person who's 'it' is gone, without telling an outright lie. So if Emilia wants to know where I am, you've got to say you think I might be with Mother in the garden. And if Mother wants to speak to me, say that you've a feeling I'm in the nursery with Dodo—and so forth, until everyone believes I'm here, even though I'm not."

Pierina clapped her hands together. "It's a lovely game!"

"I'm glad you think so."

"But are you sure there's not sin in the intention of leading others astray, just as surely as if I'd out-and-out lied?"

Alessandra smiled. "You'll make a fine scholar yet, Pierina."

"I will never be a bookworm like you—nor would I want to be! What gentleman would want to marry a girl who is always thinking?"

"A good man would! Don't forget that our own mother could read, and was said by Dante himself to recite as beautifully as anyone in all of Romagna or Lombardia."

Pierina looked suddenly sad. "I wish I could remember! My memory of her grows dimmer every day—especially since our lady took the portrait down. Sometimes I can't picture her face at all."

It was not the first time that Alessandra was sorely tempted to show Pierina the icon, which her father had made her promise to keep secret. She put her arm around

Pierina instead. "You'll remember as soon as I remind you—close your eyes!"

With Pierina's head resting on her shoulder, Alessandra described the painting their mother had sat for when she was pregnant with Dodo: a glorious half-page illumination showing the Annunciation—the very same image Fabio had copied for the icon. Alessandra looked at it so often that she could describe it perfectly, from the almond-shaped eyes to the startled brow and the slightly parted lips that seemed about to speak.

The original illumination was part of an exemplar that Carlo Giliani had been putting together to show off Old Fabio's skill and the fine quality of the books produced by their workshop.

When his wife died in childbirth, Carlo had the folio with her portrait mounted on a piece of gilt-framed wood, which he hung in a place of honor above the hearth. Later, when he married again, his new wife insisted the painting be taken down. Just that past year, Carlo had Old Fabio paint the image over again in miniature for the weighty icon he gave to Alessandra, telling her that this treasure was for her and her alone.

"You look like her, Zan-Zan," said Pierina, gazing up into her sister's wide-set, unmistakably almond-shaped brown eyes.

"Hmm. I suppose I do."

"I look more like Papa's family, don't I?"

Alessandra studied her sister's blond hair and wide blue eyes with a familiar twinge of envy. "I'm sure our stepmother feels nothing but love when she looks at you." They were both silent then, thinking about how little love their stepmother bore Alessandra. "Are you in, then? Are you going to play Disappearing with me and Nic today?"

Pierina nodded.

"Yours will be the hardest part."

"But where will you go, dressed like a boy?"

"Into my newest study hall stocked with books I've never read nor touched!"

"What are you talking about? We have the best library outside of Bologna."

Alessandra felt cheered up again, thinking about her adventure. "Ah, but this is a study hall filled not with books but the wonders of Nature—with birth and growth and death and decay, plants and creatures, earth, water, and sky."

"Are you running away?"

"Just for the day—I'll be back before supper. And if you've played your part well, no one shall ever know I was gone."

Alessandra kissed her, then scrambled up onto the windowsill. "Godspeed, Pierina!" she called out over her shoulder before steeling her nerves and jumping outside.

Four

Nicco had decided it would be best to have Alessandra ride behind him on Nero, at least at the start, until she grew enough to handle a full-size horse on her own.

She wondered if they would find a hare or a partridge, and whether Nicco would kill it—and whether she would be able to bring herself to look, rather than turn away as she often did when faced with the sight and smell of blood.

She thought of and then brushed away the memory of her mother's body split open from chest to just below the naval. She smelled the hot blood and felt her father shaking with sobs and watched between her fingers as the midwife pulled Dodo out, still in his caul.

Alessandra held on tighter to Nicco and pressed her cheek against his back, willing the image away. She felt some comfort in knowing that he, too, had been there and seen what she had seen. She closed her eyes and whispered a prayer to their mother, asking her to watch over them.

They spent that first day in the border of sunlight and gloom at the edge of the forest. Alessandra practiced climbing up and down off Nero's back, using the low branches of a tree as her ladder. She learned the proper way to tie Nero to the tree—which turned out to be the same as the bookbinder's knot she'd seen so many times before but never bothered to learn how to make. She and Nicco climbed the tree and found some feathers that Nicco said were the remains of a red falcon's meal. And Nicco told her how this was a falcon he hoped to trap one day and train to hunt with him.

They sat in the canopy of the tree, and Nicco, in a

whisper, told her everything he knew about the sounds they heard there: the names of birds, and which were good to eat and which made songs so beautiful that it would be a sin to kill them, especially now that the years of rain were over, and not nearly so many peasants were dying of hunger as before.

To both of them, the tree seemed filled with the breath of God. When they climbed down, they saw that this tree was part of a ring of trees growing around a clearing. Nicco stuck his fingers inside a mound of leaves at the base of the roots and pulled out a mushroom that was shining white and the size of Alessandra's thumb, with a slantwise cap as delicate looking as a piece of skin.

Alessandra's eyes grew even wider than they were already in the half-light of the clearing. "Isn't that—?"

"The very kind our own dear Cook once paid for with a fine, plump hen—and Father had her flavor a broth with it that he served to the Bishop."

"I saw nothing before you dug it out! How did you know it was there?"

Nicco screwed up his face, trying but failing to find the clue that had let him know. "Perhaps the way the leaves there looked a little more disturbed—but I think it's something else about things that are hidden underground. I just feel them sometimes—like heat, only it's not heat, but something else."

It was Alessandra's turn to be rapt with admiration. Her heart beat a little faster, thinking about how there might well be as many wonders beneath the surface of things as there are above, if one could but figure out how to see them.

They untied Nero and walked deeper into the woods. Nicco found the delicate skull of a vole and the scat of the bear that had eaten the animal. The horse clearly didn't like being there. "But how can he know," asked Alessandra, "that a bear was here, perhaps weeks before?"

"Because bears, like all creatures, have their pathways— and Nero no doubt smells or else somehow senses the presence of the bear, from whenever it passed by and ate this vole."

Alessandra took the clean, white, beautiful skull—as delicate as the carved ivory elephant she once saw in a stall in the marketplace in Bologna, when her mother had taken her along to buy spices. Alessandra had been allowed to hold the tiny elephant in the palm of her hand.

She wrapped the vole's beautiful little skull carefully in a broad leaf and put it in the pocket where it was most likely to stay safe and whole.

By the end of the day, she had a new respect for her brother, filthy hands, and an ache inside her to find out more. "No wonder you find Aristotle dull, Nicky! Why read about learning, when the entire world spreads its wonders at our feet?"

They ate the hunk of dried fish and two hard rolls Nicco had taken from the kitchen when Cook's back was turned. (In fact, she had seen him—but she doted particularly on the Master's elder son, and allowed him the pleasure of thinking he was outsmarting her.) Then they went to a special little place Nicco knew about, beside a stream, and gorged themselves on blackberries until their teeth were blue.

Alessandra nearly fell asleep as she rode behind her brother on the way home. She was roused by the sound of the church bells tolling Vespers, telling her that they'd stayed away too long, and that even if Pierina had played her part brilliantly, there was no way Alessandra's absence from home could have gone unmarked.

❖ ❖ ❖

Nicco pleaded ignorance about Alessandra's whereabouts when he reached the table, dirty and out of breath, midway through the meal. Pierina blushed to the roots of her blond hair.

"Well, young lady," said their father, cocking his head to one side.

Taking a big swallow of water from her goblet, Pierina nearly choked. "I thought she was with Nicco," she spluttered between coughs. "Cross my heart and hope to die!"

"Hush, child," said her stepmother. "You ought to be more careful about what you say."

Carlo Giliani glanced across the table at Nicco, who could almost look at him eye to eye now. Nicco tried his best, without any words at all, to plead with his father: *It will be bad for Alessandra if you pursue this!* He chose the biggest piece of bread on the platter at the center of the table, and then heaped some fish for himself on top of it. "My favorite sauce!" he said to no one, a little too cheerfully.

Ursula banged the flat of her palm on the table, making

the crockery tremble. "Where is your firstborn sister?"

Pierina's goblet fell to the floor, where it broke in several jagged pieces on the alternating black and white tiles.

"You will be the death of me, you three!"

"*Ecco!* Here she is," said Nicco, staring past his step-mother's head at the doorway, where Alessandra stood, dressed as herself again. She stretched and yawned in a perfect mime of sleepiness, as if she'd just woken. Her curly hair looked even more untidy than usual, and her cap was askew. Nicco could sense rather than see the rapid beating of her heart beneath her shift, as if she were a rabbit in a trap.

Ursula turned around, and Alessandra curtsied. "Forgive me, Mother"—she nodded at Ursula. "Father"—at Carlo. She had almost made it to her place at the table when Ursula grabbed her—altogether too hard—by the wrist, pulling her up short.

Alessandra looked into her stepmother's oddly amber-colored eyes, but couldn't find even one drop of love for her there. She made herself remember her mother's soft brown eyes and how they grew warmer and even darker when they lit on her, smiling and filled with love. Alessandra looked at the amber eyes and said the words, slowly and softly, inside her heart: *My mother loved me.*

"Your hands," said Ursula, her voice perfectly calm.

"Madame?"

Ursula's voice was a tad more urgent when she spoke again. "Show me your hands!"

Disengaging herself from Ursula's grasp, Alessandra shot a pleading look at her father.

"*Amore,*" he said, "the fish is getting cold."

"Your hands!" Ursula repeated in a voice as cold as the river from which the fish had been hauled up in a net that morning.

Alessandra raised her hands up and held them out, palms up. Ursula grabbed the candelabra and drew it closer to the edge of the table, dripping wax onto the white cloth.

"Turn them over!"

There was still dirt and mud and blackberry juice under Alessandra's nails. A drop of hot wax fell on the back of her hand. Alessandra flinched but didn't cry out. Another drop fell.

She thought about Aristotle's treatise on bees: how bright and shiny bees are idle—like women. (It pained her that Aristotle never had anything good to say about women!) How honey falls from the air when the stars are rising in the night sky or the rainbow rests upon the Earth. How bees produce their young from the flowers of honeysuckle, reed, and olives. She reflected on all this and wondered how the first candlemaker ever thought of embedding a wick inside a rod of beeswax to conquer the darkness of night.

Nicco shot his own dirty hands out into the wavering circle of light. "Pierina told the truth, Madame—my hands are a fair match for Alessandra's."

Pierina knelt down on the floor to gather the broken pieces of crockery.

"Leave that!" Ursula looked from one child to the other. Alessandra, still lost in thought, was staring at the beeswax on her hand—thinking how, even in the candlelight, it wedded itself to the smallest subtlety of the surface of her skin. That is how the goldsmith plies his art, she remembered—making a ring or a brooch first in wax, and then filling the place inhabited by wax with gold.

Ursula's voice was quite shrill now. "What were you doing to get such dirty hands?"

Nicco reached inside his doublet and brought out the mushroom they'd found in the forest. "We were going to give it to Cook, Madame, and it was to be a surprise for you."

Carlo Giliani's face broke into a broad smile. "By the saints!" he swore. "I didn't think I'd ever see another of those in my lifetime! Well done, Nic!"

Ursula again looked from child to child, ending with Alessandra, whose face she caressed softly, so that the girl had to look up and meet her eyes. *How*, thought Alessandra, *can the hands feel so soft when the eyes look so hard?*

"Clever girl!" Ursula said quietly, all the shrillness gone now from her voice. But her eyes bespoke mistrust of clever girls—mistrust and fear. She rang the little bell that sat at her place on the table.

The servant stepped out of the shadows to clear away the cold fish and the pile of sodden bread in the middle that would be given away as alms the following day, outside the church.

Alessandra slipped away and took her place at the long

table, between Nicco and Pierina, who wiped her saucy fingers on the tablecloth. Keeping her eyes downcast, Alessandra gave both her brother and sister a friendly pat under the table as the servant brought in a joint of meat. The food smelled good to her after her long day out of doors. She felt capable of eating the entire joint herself— and she no sooner had this thought than promised herself to confess her gluttony and repent of it at church first thing in the morning.

"Have you heard?" Ursula asked her family brightly after she'd taken her first bite of mutton on the point of her knife. "A witch is going to be burned tomorrow in the square. Alessandra, *cara*, would you pass the salt cellar, please?"

Five

Alessandra said her prayers and hung her gown, kirtle, and stockings on the rod that kept them out of reach of the mice, then jumped under the covers, next to Pierina, who was already naked.

"Get your feet away from me!" Pierina cried.

Alessandra slipped out of her chemise and put it on top of the covers with her sister's. "I'm frozen!"

"Come closer then. But not the feet—not yet!"

The two smooth and silky girls cuddled together. After a time, Pierina said, "I fear for you, Alessandra!"

"I fear for myself! That was as much as a threat tonight. Where in Persiceto has someone discovered a witch?"

"It's the old wet-nurse—the one who was convinced you were a changeling!"

"She must be even madder now than she was back then, living in that hovel at the edge of the swamp and without a friend in the world."

"The crier said she'd caused the death of three babies!"

Alessandra thought about how close she herself had come to dying by the same hand. "Did she—stab them?"

"She wasn't actually anywhere near them. But the authorities found rue in her pockets. Oh, Alessandra— they say it is the favorite plant of witches!"

"And what if that mushroom Nic found had been the favorite fungus of sorcerers? Would that make him one?"

"That's different!"

"It's only different because Nic has friends. Whereas the old wet-nurse has none."

"If her hand hadn't been stayed by our mother nearly

twelve years ago, Zan-Zan, you wouldn't be here."

What Pierina said was true. Who could Alessandra count on now to help her, if someone else imagined they saw the Devil's traces on her—or simply said so, out of jealousy or spite? Her father, who would do anything to protect her, was away so much of the time.

She nested her two feet—warm now—against Pierina's. "Sometimes I think the only thing for me is to go away."

"And then *you'd* be friendless! And with that heart of yours so stuffed with learning, you'd be accused straight-away. You mustn't! Unless—"

"Unless?"

"Unless it's to marry."

"And let myself be poked by a hairy devil of a husband who would keep me pregnant, year after year, until—"

"Don't say it!" They were both thinking about their mother—Alessandra of the grisly night of their mother's death, when her corpse was split open to release the as-yet-unbaptized Dodo so that her soul could fly to Heaven and watch over them. Pierina remembered it only as a tale, partially told to her—judiciously censored—by Nicco and

Alessandra. "Our stepmother says that I mustn't be afraid. That as many women as die in childbirth live to take joy in the baby they've brought into the world."

"And yet she has never done it."

"It is her sorrow that she herself is barren."

"I wonder," said Alessandra. "She doesn't seem particularly sorrowful to me."

"Will you go tomorrow?"

"To the burning? Certainly not. People were glad enough to heed the old woman's counsel during the years of rain and, afterwards, during the years of rot, when she could tell them which wild plants are safely eaten. How many peasant families did she save from starvation?"

"God's mercy saved them, Alessandra, as you know perfectly well!" There was a silence. "It might seem odd," Pierina ventured, "if you don't go."

"I'll spend the hours in church instead."

Pierina kissed her sister's back, just between her shoulder blades. "Good girl," she said. "That will be the safest place for you to be. Make sure someone sees you there!"

"God will see me."

"Make sure someone else sees you there."

"Go to sleep, Pierina—may the angels watch over both of us!"

"And Nicco and Dodo . . ."

"And Father . . ."

But they were both fast asleep before any other words could be spoken.

After she came back from church, Alessandra hid herself in the workshop to start reading a book her father had just borrowed from the Dominican priory. It was a newly discovered text from Avicenna, the princely Persian scholar—lately translated into Latin by a visiting monk from Toledo.

Carlo had paid a handsome price (in the form of a donation to the friars) to borrow a copy of Avicenna's treatise from the monastery, knowing that it would be much in demand at the medical school in Bologna. Old Fabio had been working such long hours on copying it— and complaining so piteously about his aching back and failing eyes—that Carlo resolved to hire another, younger artist and scribe as soon as one possessing the requisite skill could be found.

The book contained many illustrations, all of which needed to be rendered as accurately as the text. A wealthy man but still a thrifty one, Carlo regarded with horror the heavy fines levied by the University of Bologna on stationers who didn't make sure the books they published were faithfully copied from the original. Several mistakes in one year's time, and his university commission would be revoked. And where would Carlo's family be then, if this—the greater part of his livelihood, and the basis of his reputation—were taken away?

Alessandra read undisturbed until she knew she'd be missed—and then joined her family in the kitchen. All through breakfast, she pondered the words she'd read, many of which had made no sense to her at all. Was it the translation, she wondered—most likely from Persian to Hebrew and then into Latin—that rendered the words so difficult to parse? Or was it the nature of the thoughts themselves?

After the meal, she waited until everyone else had left the kitchen—and then walked across the passageway, back into her father's scriptorium.

It was a threefold treat for her senses, going from the fragrance of cloves and roasted meat and woodsmoke to the blast of cold, sage-scented air in the stone passageway to the sweet smell of ink and the acrid, sulfurous tang of the *gesso* being mixed by the latest set of apprentices, two eight-year-old twin boys from Lombardy.

She walked up quietly behind Old Fabio to watch him as he hunkered over the vellum folio, applying gold leaf to an illumination of the Adoration of the Magi. The set of pages were part of a commission for a Little Book of Hours her father had won after an evening of drinking with the Bishop. Dank early mornings were the best, she'd heard, for the application of gold leaf—and this was just such a morning.

Old Fabio used the gilder's tip to pick up a piece of gold that had been pounded so thin that it was practically not of the material world anymore. Alessandra didn't dare even breathe as he let it float down to the red silk gilder's cushion, where it settled like a shimmering slick of precious oil.

"May I blow it flat?" she whispered.

"Madonna mia!" said the illuminator, nearly jumping out of his chair. "I thought you were the Angel of Death, come to take me!"

"I'm sorry!"

"And look what you've made me do! The gold has floated away."

"It's here," said Alessandra, from her hands and knees on the floor. "May I have the gilder's brush, *Maestro*?"

Old Fabio clucked his tongue but gave her the tool, as he knew his knees were too stiff to allow him to go searching underneath his desk. "Don't break it!"

Alessandra touched the tiny brush to the escaped piece of pounded gold, as delicate as an insect's wing. She cupped her other hand around it and held her breath as she dropped it onto the bloodred silk of the tiny cushion. "There it is."

The illuminator raised his chin to look at her. "Well done, *Signorina*."

Alessandra smiled. She liked being good at things—especially things she wasn't expected to be good at.

"Blow on it, if you want to—but gently!"

The little wrinkles in the golden wing were smoothed out in the current of Alessandra's warm breath. Old Fabio took his knife and cut a crescent out from it for the Christ child's halo. "Breathe harder now on the place on the page where it goes—just there. Breathe on the infant Jesus."

Alessandra blew her warm breath on Christ to make the pink, crescent-shaped spot of *gesso* around his head soft enough to receive the gold. Then she pulled back and watched, holding her breath, while the gold came floating down from the gilder's brush, seeming to jump into place, as if it knew exactly where it belonged. Old Fabio covered it quickly with a piece of silk and pushed on the halo with his cracked and blackened thumb.

"Finish it up, if you want to try." He handed her the burnishing tool, a dog's tooth mounted on a wooden handle. "Delicate but strong—there's the way."

Alessandra stood over the folio in which the Christ child had suddenly come to life.

"You've a good hand, my girl. You could do any job in this workshop and do it well. Not like that brother of yours!"

Alessandra looked at her hands, a child's hands still, smooth and dimpled and as yet unmarked by life. She was glad they were good hands. She breathed on them in the cold morning air of the workshop, as if they too would suddenly shine gold with the certainty of her own future and whatever brightness it held.

Alessandra was careful, after the grim bonfire in the square and the flesh-scented days following, to please her stepmother—at least, to the extent that Ursula would allow herself to be pleased by her least favorite among her husband's children.

Carlo left for several days on a business trip to Bologna, and Ursula took advantage of his absence to give Alessandra tasks she would never dare give her otherwise. So while Pierina sat by the kitchen fire, helping Cook put up apples to dry, Alessandra was sent to the well with the two buckets balanced, one at each end of the rod that hurt her back and neck even while the buckets were empty.

It was one thing for the servant, who was broad and well padded and could have fit two of Alessandra inside her, to fetch the water. But Alessandra embraced the task without complaint, taking it as an intellectual as well as a physical challenge.

Nicco caught her as she crouched beneath the weight

of the two full buckets, her back to the well, hanging on tight with both hands to the rod that was braced across her shoulders. He stopped her just as she was about to use her fanny to shove the well bucket, tied to the rod as a counterbalance, over the edge and into the well.

"Are you trying to drown yourself? Surely there's an easier way."

Alessandra picked herself up from the ground, where she'd fallen after Nicco untied the rope and the counterweight was gone. "I'm trying to haul water, as I've been ordered."

"Who would dare order a shrimp like you to carry the water?"

"Who do you think?"

Nicco, broad shouldered and well built for a lad of fourteen, grunted as he lifted the full buckets in the air and let the rod come to rest behind his head, holding on to the ends with his meaty hands. "You should have called me."

"I thought I could devise a way to do it myself."

Nicco grinned. "The world will be a better place because of you, Alessandra, if you're able to stay alive long enough to do even half of what you cook up inside that brilliant heart of yours."

As they walked along, Alessandra brushed absently at the water sloshing over her from the closest bucket. "Don't you wonder, Nic, how the rest of our body hears our thoughts as the heart thinks them, and knows what to do?"

"Why should I bother myself about such a bloody stupid thing?" Nic grunted again as he lowered the brace of buckets onto the kitchen threshold.

Ursula was standing in the doorway when they opened it, as if she'd been waiting for them. "I told Alessandra to fetch the water."

"Yes, you did, Madame!" Nicco put his arm around his sister's shoulder. "It made as much sense as it would for me to put my saddle on my dog and try to ride him."

"Do you dare defy me, Niccolò?" Ursula was a tall woman, but not quite as tall as Nicco. She raised herself up to her full height and held her head high as she spoke to him.

"Know, Madame, that I will defend my sister if anyone misuses her."

He and Ursula stared at each other, neither hazarding to utter another word. Alessandra, roused from her own thoughts, looked up at them, from face to face, locked in combat as surely as if they'd been trading blows.

"Have an apple, anyone?" Pierina piped up from the fire. When Nicco and Ursula continued to glare at each other, unmoving, she added in a smaller voice, "They're awfully nice this year."

The dog started barking, there was the sound of horses, and the servant ran out from the stable. Carlo, accompanied by a stranger, was back from Bologna.

Two riders came abreast of the house, the master on his high horse and someone unknown riding a brindled donkey. When the stranger removed his cloak and hood, it was clear that he was not much more than a boy, though he looked tall—about the same age and height, in fact, as Nicco.

"Husband," Ursula said, lowering her eyes, perhaps to conceal the anger in them.

"By God!" Carlo bellowed. "It's good to be home." He reached down to chuck Alessandra under the chin. "Are those tears, my pet?"

Alessandra took his cloak, freeing him to fold her in his arms. "All is well, Papa."

"Nicco? It's going well, my boy?" They clasped each other by the shoulder.

"Have you brought a new playmate for us, Father?" Nicco said with a friendly smile for the boy on the donkey.

Carlo laughed—it was a sound that filled his children with the conviction that all was right with the world. He slapped the parcel that seemed about to burst the seams of the saddlebag. "I've brought the text and drawings for a fine, new medical book we're going to publish, plus a scribe and artist who will please Old Fabio mightily. This is Giorgio da Padova, a newly minted journeyman, and as fine an illuminator as I've seen in many years."

Pierina had by then come out from the kitchen and was wiping her hands on her apple-stained apron. "Giorgio da Padova," she said dreamily.

"Are you a parrot?" snapped Ursula. "Excuse our rudeness, young sir. We are simple country folk here." Ursula held herself beautifully tall, with a bearing to dispel anyone's notion that she was anything other than the wife of a rich and powerful man. "Welcome to our home."

He began to answer her—he opened his mouth to answer her. But the words wouldn't come, so that Alessandra wondered if the lad was mute. He reddened as they waited for his reply, as he opened his mouth and closed it again. He reminded Alessandra of a hungry bird. And then he managed to speak, although it was little more than a stammer and the words took ages to come out of him, and only with the greatest difficulty, as if he were cold and shivering. "I t-t-t-thank y-y-y-you, m-m-m-y l-l-l-l—!"

"Well," interrupted Ursula, looking quizzically at her husband. "We will not worry about you chattering idly instead of working."

Giorgio looked as if he wanted to answer, but only smiled instead.

"Welcome, Giorgio!" said Nicco, helping him off his donkey and patting him on the back. "I expect you'd like a wash and a rest after that long ride."

Six

Carlo was right: Giorgio da Padova's skill as a miniaturist was astonishing. And he not only made charming decorations, rich in color and detail, but added an element that no other illuminator had ever attempted in the workshop before: He gathered things from the natural world and painted them in such a lifelike way, in the borders and twining around the fancy first letters, that one had to look twice and even touch the page to assure oneself that these were only drawings of ivy and wild strawberries, fern fronds and mussel shells, and not the real things.

Carlo hoped to institute another innovation with the addition of Giorgio to his workshop. Some copies of books were being made now in which each separate folio was numbered sequentially. The thing took a lot of planning, putting the numbers on the pages before they were cut up and assembled. But students—especially those in the law school—were extolling the superior merits of these books, in which a given part of the text could be referred to and found again and again, even by someone who had never read the book before. This "pagination," as it was called, also improved the system whereby authorized editions of books were divided into pieces and rented out to students for copying. To know where one had left off and was to begin again saved any amount of confusion and wasted time.

Old Fabio had sworn that he'd never consent to number pages, calling it the work of the Devil. But this Giorgio—young and open as the young are to new ideas—had simply narrowed his eyes, thinking it over for a moment, then smiled brightly at his new master. The trick, he knew, would be to paginate the books he worked on without offending Old Fabio.

Alessandra and Nicco took double delight in their outings together now, when they were able to slip away, looking for ever more admirable objects to bring back for Giorgio to copy. And unlike Old Fabio, Giorgio could really be a friend to them, always ready with a smile and happy to listen to their talk when he was working on artwork rather than text. Fabio always went home to eat dinner at his own house, with his old wife, who was as wrinkled as one of last winter's apples. Whatever apprentices were in the workshop boarded with him and his wife, where Fabio could keep a strict eye on them.

But Giorgio slept in an alcove near the workshop fire and was invited every day to dine at his master's table, sitting as often as not wedged comfortably on the bench between Nicco and Pierina.

Walking undetected into the workshop one day while Giorgio was there alone, Pierina was astonished to overhear him singing—in a rich, warm, and winsome voice—without stammering at all.

The sense of betrayal she felt was awful. How the entire family had coddled him and petted him. How they had trusted and confided in him! "I can't believe it!

You—of such goodness and honesty. You've been deceiving us all this time!"

"I—I—I—," began Giorgio.

"Oh, stop it, stop it!" Pierina held her hands over her ears. "How can you think me so stupid?"

Blushing and stammering both, Giorgio finally managed to say that his ability to sing without stammering was a mystery he couldn't account for.

The process of telling his story took time—and a great deal of patience on Pierina's part. But the telling and the hearing of that story was the start of a powerful bond between them.

Giorgio had always stammered, ever since he could remember. And he had always been able to sing without stammering at all. Because he had first sung in church, the thing was counted as proof of his vocation for the priesthood. But he knew—and his friends knew—that he could sing without stammering even if he was singing a bawdy drinking song.

Once the secret was out, Pierina and her siblings went to great lengths to coerce or trick Giorgio into singing, as all of them reveled in the marvel of the fluency of his voice when raised in song.

He could be counted on to sing when he wanted to say something quickly—as when Dodo was about to touch an illumination that was not yet dry, or when one of the apprentices nearly trod on a cache of hen's eggs, destined for tempera, wrapped in a piece of linen. Both picture and eggs would have been spoilt if Giorgio had taken the time he would have needed to speak his warning.

Pierina, who also loved to sing, suddenly found excuses to spend time in the workshop—a place that had held little enough attraction for her previously, when Old Fabio was the only artist there. She would come down from the second floor of the house with a basket of beans to shell or a bit of embroidery she was working on.

When Ursula demanded to know why she had to go downstairs to do her needlework, Pierina would use the excuse that she was copying one of Giorgio's designs. She was usually able to get Giorgio to sing a *caccia* with her, alternating, depending on who knew the song best, who was the leader and who the follower. Sometimes the other scribes chimed in, and then the workshop was a merrier place than it had ever been before. If students were there copying, they either joined the song or roundly told the singers to shut up, depending on the text they were working on and the mood it had put them in.

Carlo understood that he'd found a gem in this young illuminator, whose work had already been much in demand when he was a freelance illustrator and scribe in Bologna. With two accomplished artists in his employ, Carlo could seize the opportunities that abounded now, between the rapidly growing call for textbooks and the rising number of nobles and other wealthy families who counted books—lavishly illustrated and gorgeously bound—as a mark of wealth and status. As treasures to be passed on from one generation to the next, right there alongside the family jewels.

One morning in August, Carlo sent the children out to gather oak apples, the small, hard, fruitlike tumors that grow on the trunks and branches of oak trees. Slowly cooked in water and mixed with ferrous earth from Spain, the ground-up oak galls made for an excellent and free supply of black ink. A long-sought-after commission for a Book of Hours for Romeo Pepoli (destined as a wedding present for his nephew's bride-to-be) had tripled the demand for ink in the Giliani workshop, and a great new batch was needed right away. The apprentices and all the servants were busy mixing pigment, making *gesso*, and scraping parchment—and so the four children were pressed into service.

Nicco was happy, as the day of gathering oak apples meant that he was excused from his morning lessons.

Even Emilia had been pressed into service in the workshop that day, and fretted because the children would have no one to look after them but Nicco. She sent him off with strict instructions to watch out for any riders wearing the colors of the Guelfs, who had lately arrested two men of the Ghibelline party in a nearby town. Nicco rolled his eyes but nonetheless promised Emilia to sound the hunting horn if they were in distress, watch over the girls, and make sure Dodo wasn't stung by any late-emerging wasps that hadn't yet flown from the galls that served as their nurseries.

"Why is we Ghibellines?" Dodo wanted to know as they made their way down the dusty pathway, the autumn air filled with the smell of dry leaves and woodsmoke.

"We're with the Emperor," explained Pierina, "while the Guelfs are the Pope's party."

"You know," said Alessandra, "it does seem odd, doesn't it? I asked Papa, and he said it's ever been the same, even before our great-great-grandparents were born. The Pope's men and the Emperor's men, battling it out, killing each other for hundreds of years. And still there's always a new Emperor, when the old one dies, and always a new Pope, and nothing changes."

"Keeps everyone busy," said Nicco.

They walked down to the stand of oak trees that grew near the post road, past the margins of their land, and looked all around them for riders or even the dust of riders.

But there was no one on the road, neither Guelfs nor Ghibellines. There was only the sound of cicadas and, occasionally—to their great relief—the wind in the trees.

Nicco hiked Dodo up onto his shoulders, from where he could reach higher than any of them, while Pierina and Alessandra guided him from down below. The oak apples that were not yet ready for gathering were still inhabited by wasps.

"Not that one, Dodo!" said Alessandra when she saw him reaching for one that still looked full. "Get the one that has a hole in it, right next to it!"

"Eek—not that one!" said Pierina. "The wasp is just coming out!"

Domenico, a sensible boy even at the tender age of four, pulled his hand away.

Nicco put his brother back on the ground and climbed up into the lower branches of the tree. "Hold the basket over your head, Zan!" He stripped the hard, silvery gray fruits, the size of small, misshapen plums, off the leaves and twigs by the handful. They fell into the basket with the sound of hail. "Ouch!"

"Did you get stung?" said Pierina.

"It's nothing."

"Come down," said Alessandra. "Let's put some mud on it."

"I'll get some of these lower ones," Pierina urged. "Do come down!"

Nicco gave in to his sisters' tender ministrations and jumped to the ground. "Can you see the stinger?"

Pierina, who liked to think her brother loved her best,

grabbed Nicco's injured hand. "Move over, Zan—you're blocking the light!"

"Wasps don't drop their stinger—just their poison." Pushing Pierina aside, Alessandra brought Nicco's hand up to her mouth, sucked on the swelling there, and then spat. "Let's put some mud on it now."

Pierina was torn between jealousy and admiration for her sister. "We should get you a pair of red gloves, Alessandra—and then you could go about the parish, selling cures."

Nicco added, "And sniffing the urine of everyone who complains of feeling ill."

"And casting their horoscope!" Pierina was terribly glad that Nic seemed to be taking her part.

Alessandra, ignoring both of them, was digging around the roots of the tree, looking for some damp earth.

"Are you going to do it or not, Zan? It hurts like hell."

Done teasing, Pierina knelt down beside her sister. "What are you looking at?"

"This." Alessandra's digging had revealed another oak apple, much like the others. But this one was growing out of the roots of the tree. She dropped it when she felt something moving about inside it.

All four knelt down to watch a wasp crawl out of the little hole in the dry gall, and walk on its insect legs up the roots toward the trunk of the tree.

Nicco scooped up a little mud and put it over the place where he'd been stung. "Hell of a doctor you'd make, Alessandra!" He made to tromp on the wasp, but Alessandra pushed his foot aside.

"Look at it, Nic! It doesn't have any wings."

"Well, neither do we, in case you haven't noticed. We have to get a move on, if we're to make it back on time for dinner."

While they were trudging home, with the baskets full and their hands stained brown, Alessandra suggested they stop in the orchard to pick up a fig branch that could be used to stir the oak apples while they soaked in the sun— and to eat a few figs, if there were any ripe ones.

"Hush!" said Pierina. They heard the sound of hooves along the road. "Can you make out their colors?"

Nicco, who had the best eyes among them, squinted

into the distance. "They're neither one nor the other faction. They're—" He picked up his basket. "Hurry up, you three! They're traders! Let's go see what they've got for us!"

The traders had come all the way from La Magna. What they had turned out to be lapis lazuli, brought over a year of traveling by camel and horse, passed from the hand of one herdsman to another and paid for in blood and gold, all the way from the mountain caliphates of Greater Khorasan. Carlo was beside himself with happiness. This was just in time for the prodigious need they were going to have for aquamarine. He'd been prepared to scrape the pigment off any old manuscripts he could get his hands on, so rare was the gemstone these days, with so many brigands along the roads and so many people willing to pay such a high price for the only color befitting the Virgin's robes and the skies of Heaven. He made the traders promise to pass his way again the following year.

Yes, he was sure that his fortune was made now and his children would be safe. This was a sign from God.

❖ ❖ ❖

It seemed to Alessandra that Ursula had loosened her hold on her or, much to her delight, had somehow forgotten about her. She grew enough that year to ride the little gelding kept by Carlo's groom. She never learned to ride as well as Nicco—but, still, she learned to ride well enough and to wear her brother's clothes with such confidence that the neighbors—always alert to anything new—took her for an apprentice or cousin or some other young male hanger-on at the Gilianis'.

Alessandra was learning about the world of Nature from her brother, and how to draw from Giorgio, and she continued to read whenever light and time allowed. Her heart was full and her cheeks were rosy, and a happier girl could not have been found in the province when the family gathered around the table on her saint's name day, to celebrate the end of her thirteenth year.

Ursula, smiling with uncharacteristic serenity, raised her goblet to Alessandra.

"Fourteen," she said, taking a sip of her wine. "The age when girls must be kept inside."

Alessandra felt herself go pale.

"The age," continued Ursula, still smiling, "when girls

must be kept even from looking out windows or doors. When they must be kept safely apart from all young men." Here she looked at Nicco. "Even their brothers."

"*Amore*," said Carlo. "Where do you get these ideas?"

"From the Holy Father," said Ursula. "It is my duty to protect your daughter's virtue, and I will see that it is done. No matter what—" Here she looked at all of them, one by one. "No matter what anyone says, as God is my witness!"

Alessandra never appreciated her freedom until it was taken away. Her father's house—so long a haven of learning and a source of comfort—was transformed by her stepmother's zealous oversight into a barrier between Alessandra and all the wonders and pleasures of the outside world.

Nicco and Pierina could come and go as they pleased, so long as they got their work done. Even Dodo, free to romp unsupervised in the garden, was allowed more license than Alessandra. Ursula barred her from the scriptorium, citing the frequent presence of students there—and made sure she kept Alessandra occupied with housework, far from the schoolroom, when Nicco had his lessons.

Once a week, Alessandra was allowed to go to Confession—but always with Ursula, proud and showy in a velvet gown, walking close enough to hear what anyone else might try to say to her. So large was Ursula's shadow that Alessandra felt her own physical presence in the world diminishing, like sandstone being worn away by wind and rain.

Reading was her only solace. She read whatever she could bribe or beg someone else to bring to her—and sometimes she wrote her thoughts in a book of spoiled sheets of vellum that Giorgio gathered and bound for her. Pierina stole ink and tiny brushes for her, too, so that Alessandra could practice sketching. For want of another model, she drew her own hands, her naked feet, and the ancient twisting vines of the wisteria that grew outside her window. She thought about the surface of living things, and how their shape came from everything hidden inside.

The summer spread its glorious wings while Alessandra was locked indoors. The first few months passed quickly enough in the pleasures she found in reading and drawing—but then the autumn came.

Her father was away, searching out new books to pub-lish, making his yearly rounds to the greatest libraries of the region, in monasteries and noble palaces. Ursula took advantage of his absence to say things she never would have dared say when he was at home.

Quite capable of being pleasant and even charming when she wanted to, Ursula made it clear—day after day, in a relentless stream of cruel comments—that Alessandra's ongoing presence in the household was the only thing that stood between Ursula and perfect domestic bliss. Alessandra was selfish and horrid for refusing to marry or take the veil and leave Ursula in peace to enjoy her husband's other children.

While her stepmother kept watch on her, Alessandra sat and sewed seed pearls on yards and yards of blue silk that Ursula said would one day serve as the cloth of her wedding gown. No field was ever sowed so thickly—nor were there ever seeds with less chance of sprouting. As Alessandra plied the needle, poking it up through the silk and through the pearl and down again, she thought about the smell of dry leaves and ripe pears, and the sounds of the harvest songs wafting across the parched fields. She looked down at her white hands and remembered how they were stained purple the year before, when she and Nicco stole into the vineyard and feasted on the blackest, ripest grapes they could find. She learned to answer Ursula without really hearing what she said, making the small, polite sounds considered fitting conversation for girls.

The more she stayed indoors alone, while her siblings climbed trees and swam in the river and watched the sunsets, the more Alessandra grew to loathe her jailor. Fall slipped away from her, barely glimpsed—and then the fog and rain of winter came. By then—even though her father was home again—each day seemed to last a year. Her eyes ached from the needlework, and her head hurt so much that even Ursula sometimes took pity on her.

When she was allowed to lie in bed in her room, Alessandra looked at the square of sky that showed outside her window and dreamed of doorways.

The following spring, Alessandra's father came to visit her in her room, where she lay in bed reading after the midday meal. The covers were pulled up around her shoulders.

There was a fire burning in the brazier. Outside, the rain was falling, although Alessandra could only tell from the silver droplets that sat like pearls in the silver of her father's hair.

"Look what I've brought you, Curly-top!" He opened his fur-lined cloak and brought out a baby rabbit, which peeked out from between his fingers and wriggled its nose at Alessandra.

She smiled at it from over the top edge of her book. "Dear Papa, you're always trying to tempt me away from my reading, aren't you?" She marked her place with the striped tail feather from a hawk—a souvenir of Nicco's latest outing to the forest—then lay the book down beside her. "What a lovely little bit of life and fluff! Was it its mother we ate today?"

"Cook saved this one for you. His brothers and sisters, I'm afraid, have been made into a stew."

Alessandra took the bunny from her dad and stroked it gently with her cheek. "How its little heart is pounding!"

"I want to speak to you about a matter of importance," said Carlo, settling himself onto the cushions that covered the long chest beside his daughter's bed.

Alessandra kissed the baby rabbit and put it in her sleeve, from where it peeked out, wriggling its silken ears as if still unable to believe its good fortune, landing here in this luxurious bedroom instead of in the stew pot.

"You know how much I treasure you, daughter."

"Thank you, Papa. But you make me tremble with fear now, as this can only be the preamble to a piece of bad news."

Carlo sighed. "You have ever been two steps ahead of everyone else in this household, Alessandra. Your first nanny was convinced you were a changeling—"

"And would have killed me with her knife, if Mother hadn't snatched it from her hands and sent her packing!"

As Carlo looked at his daughter—so like his late wife in her face as well as her spirit—he was filled with love for both of them. "I'm leaving for France, soon—not an unusually long trip, but a dangerous one."

He glanced away from her, sighed, and spoke more quietly than before. "It is time to get you a husband."

When Alessandra said nothing—seeming to hold her breath as she stared at him, as if trying to read in his face the greater truth of his words—he added, his voice weighed down by his own unhappiness over the matter, "I promised I'd tell you today."

She spoke in a whisper. "Have I already been promised to someone?"

Carlo, in his turn, was silent.

"It's true, then!" Alessandra's voice broke when she spoke again. "Could it not be deferred, Papa?"

Carlo shook his head. "The papers have already been drafted."

"Burn them—I beg you!"

Feeling sorry with all his heart for letting himself be so influenced by his wife, Carlo took his daughter's hands in his. "Although you are blessed with a mighty intelligence, Alessandra, you are yet an innocent child." He reached out and gently touched her cheek, then used his thumb to wipe away a tear. "Have you thought about what your life would be like if something were to happen to me?"

Alessandra threw her arms around him. "Nothing will happen to you, my dearest Papa! You are strong and well."

"And old and gray," he said, gently pushing her away.

"Now, I want you to think hard, Alessandra, about things that may not please you."

She nodded, although her bottom lip quivered.

"When I die—"

"Stop, Papa! I won't hear of it!"

"You will, child! Now be brave and hear me out. When I die, your stepmother will depend on Nicco—at least until she marries again."

"Oh, stop—I can't stand it!"

"Hush, Alessandra! Listen to me. Nicco will have his place here, as will Pierina, who is a girl more in your stepmother's mold. And Dodo has never known any other mother. But you, Alessandra—"

"I know. She's told me often enough: I am a thorn in her side. A ghost here to haunt her. Uninterested in the things that interest her, and excited by things that no girl has the right or need to know."

Carlo patted his daughter's hand. "She fears you outshine her."

"I have no desire to do so! I wish she'd simply leave me alone!"

"She cannot do that, Alessandra, and neither can I. We

must think of the welfare of all four of our children."

"Oh, Papa, you know she wishes I were dead!"

"Hush, child! She only wishes to see you well situated in life."

"Away from her!" Alessandra looked into her father's kind blue eyes, the color of cornflowers and so like Pierina's. "Away from all of you."

Carlo looked suddenly older and more tired than he had just a moment before. "You've read every book in our library now."

"Not yet!" said Alessandra. "And there are many I wish to read again. I was too green in my understanding when I read them the first time."

"You are, in truth, my daughter."

"I am, Papa." She made to put her arms around him again, and in the process sent the baby rabbit flying. Carlo—whom Alessandra had once seen catch a thrush midair—deftly caught the terrified little thing and restored it to the safe haven of his daughter's sleeve.

"Please," she begged him. "Buy me some time!"

"I must keep peace in this household, Alessandra. And as unpleasant a thing as it is to admit, I think you would receive fairer treatment by the hearth of a man who would love and cherish you as your stepmother never will."

She grabbed his hands again and made him look at her. "I have a plan, Papa—a great and half-mad hope! But it cannot be fulfilled for another year. And it can never be fulfilled if I am married."

"Will you take the veil, my girl?"

"If only it were such an easy path!" Alessandra shook her head. "You know how I hate being locked up—and how limited the curriculum is at the cloister." She looked at the pair of finches her father had given her to ease the tedium of living indoors. She didn't tell him, for fear of giving offense, that she took small comfort in the caged creatures, only seeing in their plight a reminder of her own.

"You are silent, Alessandra. Will you not confide in me?"

"Not yet. Just promise me you'll throw those papers in the fire! Promise me, Papa!"

"I cannot promise you that—"

"Please!"

"Hush! But perhaps I could convince her to wait a bit, on grounds of finding an even more powerful match for you—a gentleman with a name that would give your stepmother cause to hold her head even higher."

"If it would buy me time, you could betroth me to the King of China, for all I care! Just so long as I can make my way to Bologna before he comes to claim me."

"Bologna?" Carlo looked at his daughter as if she indeed might be the changeling she'd been accused of being so long ago. "There is only one sort of unmarried woman who makes it her business to stay in Bologna."

"Fie, Papa! How can you think so ill of me?" Alessandra buried her face in her hands.

Carlo reached out and stroked his daughter's hair. "Will you not confide in me, Alessandra?" he said again.

She sniffed and wiped her face, smoothing the covers around her to stall for time. To seem as tall as possible, she sat up straighter, hoping that the nobility of her purpose would shine through her words. Silently, she prayed to the soul of her mother to intercede for her and aid her cause—her mother, whose needless death had inspired Alessandra's ambition, and whose love had given her the belief that it might, against all odds, be possible to fulfill.

And then she said what she'd practiced saying a hundred times, never finding quite the right way. She let the words tumble out of her, unplanned, all in a jumble. "I want to go to the University of Bologna, Papa. I want to study medicine."

Seven

Carlo looked at his daughter a long time before responding to the astonishing thing she'd just said. He knew that she was not like any other child, male or female, he'd ever known. But this newest conceit of hers left him quite speechless.

She spoke when he said nothing. "There are female scholars in the town."

"Are there?" Carlo looked thoughtful. "Are you sure?"

Alessandra was longing to say yes, of course she was sure—but, in truth, she didn't know. Now that she thought about it, the few female scholars she'd ever read about had all been high-ranking nuns from noble families, or noblewomen who were tutored at home. "Females, I believe, can attend lectures if they so desire. At least, I have never heard any injunction against it." Her voice trailed off into uncertainty.

"And medicine, child! What man would surrender his pulse and his urine to a female physician?"

"I want to study the workings of the body, Father—not to wear the red gloves and attend the ill."

"Will you learn only from books, then? Because I can and will procure whatever books you want, and you can study them here at your leisure. . . ." He gestured around the warm and cozy room with its bed as commodious as a throne, well padded with embroidered pillows and hung about with curtains, now pulled back to let in the light. "In the safety and tranquillity of your own home."

Alessandra looked around her room, taking in all her father had done to make it a whole world for her since her stepmother had clipped her wings, keeping her imprisoned here as surely as the finches in their wicker cage. "I want to study as Aristotle says men should study."

"Men, Alessandra, not girls."

"It's true the old Stagirite has nothing kind to say about the intellectual capacity of females. But I am living proof that he was biased in his view!"

Carlo thought how proud his daughter was—how proud and pretty and, he had to admit, correct in her opinion. She had all the capacity required to pursue any of the seven liberal arts: grammar, logic, rhetoric, arithmetic, geometry, music, or even astronomy. Nicco, for all his lovable manly bluster, was as a lowly apprentice, not even worthy of holding a candle to his sister's intellectual pursuits. She was a natural scholar and an original thinker. Was it not but an unhappy accident that she was born a girl?

And yet she was a girl, and what she asked for was against every law of man and Nature. "Wouldn't music be better suited to you, Alessandra? Both the study of music and the study of medicine are concerned, after all, with achieving harmony."

"And yet they are as different as an angel is from a living creature, Papa! I want to study the body itself and learn the secrets of how it works—of everything that's hidden beneath the flesh. To learn, as Aristotle teaches us to do, by observation."

"Alessandra, you have been shut up in this room too long—you need fresh air!"

"There is a doctor who teaches at the University of Bologna. He chooses assistants from among the best students in the medical school. I know you've heard of him—his little book has been much in demand for copying since its publication last year."

"Anatomia?"

"The very one! Mondino de' Liuzzi. Our Giorgio did some of the pictures for him. Each illuminator was sworn to secrecy, as they used corpses as models—" Alessandra clapped her hand over her mouth, realizing what she'd just done. "You won't tell, Papa, will you? They only use corpses from the gallows or the hospitals, and never the bodies of people from hereabouts."

Carlo was by now weeping. Alessandra stopped herself from saying more, enfolding herself in his arms, as soon as she saw the effect of her words.

"Have I not ever shown you love and kindness, Alessandra, and given you everything you desire?"

"Of course you have, dear Papa!"

"Did I nurture you and coddle and encourage you, only to see you banished from the company of every decent, God-fearing person? To see you become a smut in the eye of God Himself?"

Alessandra stiffened, hearing an unpleasant echo of her stepmother's diction in her father's words, even as she let herself be held by him. She pushed him gently away and dried her eyes. "New things are being learned all the time—especially now that so many of the ancient texts from the Greeks and the Arabs are more widely accessible—and largely because of you and your brother stationers, Papa!"

"Woe betide me, then!"

Alessandra caught and held his eyes. "Do you never think that if someone, somewhere had bothered to learn and study more, Mother might still be alive today?"

"Oh, my dear child—God calls us to Him when and how He will."

"And yet you physic me when I have the ague, and Emilia makes Dodo take cod-liver oil, and you have always done your best to keep your children safe and healthy. Is that going against God's will?"

"*Basta*, Alessandra—enough!" Carlo held out his palm to keep her from saying more. "You cannot go to Bologna to study medicine. You must not even think about it anymore." Carlo shook his head when she was silent, simply looking at him with those brown eyes of hers that were so like her mother's—eyes filled now with reproach. "Your stepmother will never allow it—and although I am ruler of this family, still it is in my interest to keep my wife in good humor."

"At my expense?"

"How you vex me, Alessandra! What you're asking is unreasonable! No girl of Persiceto has ever gone off to study in Bologna. And females are not permitted to compete for advanced degrees. You would heap shame upon our heads—and even Pierina's chances of marrying well would be compromised."

"It is not fair!"

"It is the way of this world, daughter."

That night, after everyone else in the house was sleeping, Alessandra took her candle and stole into the storeroom, where she took her treasure out of its hiding place, prayed, and kissed the image of her mother's face again and again.

The cold stone of the floor seemed to grow warmer and softer beneath her knees. And in the candlelight, after many *Ave Marias*, she saw a golden web cast itself like a veil over the face of the Virgin.

Alessandra barely managed to keep the heavy icon in her trembling hands. Was it a sign to her? Her mother's blessing?

She hugged the icon to her breast, crossed herself, and tucked her treasure away again, well hidden beneath her mother's clothes.

Through all that spring, Alessandra uncomplainingly did the household tasks her stepmother assigned to her, and spent the rest of the time propped up in her bed, reading and thinking.

It was a breathtakingly beautiful spring, filled with birdsong and blossoms. Alessandra experienced what she could from Pierina's tales of the world beyond her little room, and basked in the sunlight and fresh air on the way to and from church. She walked slowly, soaking up as much as she could of the sights, sounds, and sweet scents of the outdoors.

Pierina proved to be more than willing to smuggle books or parts of books in progress out of the scriptorium. But as luscious spring turned again to tantalizing summer, she was increasingly annoyed with the obedient lump that seemed to be standing in for her once rebellious, unquenchably adventurous sister.

Pierina shared a room with Dodo now—it was part of Ursula's plan to keep Alessandra untainted by worldly things and thus as grandly marriageable as possible.

Nonetheless, Pierina often slipped into her sister's bed at night, as Dodo kicked and snored and kept her awake.

On one such night, she entered Alessandra's room in the wee hours, surprised to find her sister writing in a little notebook that was visible for but an instant before Alessandra whisked the book under the covers and blew out the candle.

Pierina felt her way in the dark, careful not to bark her shins on the chest beside Alessandra's bed. She climbed over it and slipped underneath the covers. "What are you writing," she whispered, "at this late hour?"

"Why are you bothering me, *moscerino*?"

"And so I'm a gnat now, am I?" Pierina sulked.

"It's hot," said Alessandra. "Move away from me." Pierina was feeling around under the covers for the book. "Get out! Leave me be!"

"I won't!" Pierina turned her back to Alessandra and they lay like that, bottom to bottom. They could hear the whisper of bats flying in and out of the open window, hunting for mosquitoes.

Alessandra turned on her other side and stroked a lock of Pierina's hair aside and then whispered into her ear. "You're a lovable gnat, at any rate."

"I hate you!"

"Hush—don't hate me."

"You hide everything from me now! What's happened to you, Zan-Zan?" Pierina's voice was hoarse with anger. "I want my sister back!"

Despite the heat, Alessandra drew Pierina into her arms. "You have me still, *moscerino*."

Pierina made Alessandra turn and face her. "Nicco says that you and Papa have some plan afoot. And our step-mother sighs contentedly all the time now, and has called on the silk merchant twice to show her his wares. But Nicco says he's sure you have no intention of marrying, and Giorgio thinks I may be right in thinking you plan to take the veil."

Alessandra felt the sting of being spoken of behind her back by those she'd counted as her allies. It was almost as if she'd left them already. "You know as well as I do of our stepmother's desire to send me away," she began stiffly. "And, of course, as a dutiful daughter, I must—"

Pierina interrupted her. "Say nothing! Say nothing rather than shutting me out again!"

The heat of her words did a good deal to soften Alessandra's resolve. "Oh, little sister—my sweet pest of a little sister! Do you remember our game of Disappearing?"

"I remember that it got us in a great deal of trouble."

"Well, I've refined the rules somewhat—and the game, I'm quite sure, will work better this time. But in case it doesn't, I'm not involving you and Nic. I'm taking the risks, as well I should, entirely upon myself."

"We are a family, Alessandra, and any risk you take upon yourself will redound upon us all."

It annoyed Alessandra that her sister, so often selfish and frivolous, was also sometimes right.

She lay there through much of that night, while Pierina softly snored, and wondered what it was inside her that made her long for an unlit pathway and places that no girl from Persiceto had ever seen before. She knew she would take such a path. But how she would find the means to sustain herself was still a problem that nagged at her, kept her awake, and haunted her dreams when she finally fell asleep.

When the pears and pomegranates hung ripe upon the trees, Ursula gave a banquet in honor of Alessandra's fifteenth name day.

Even though no one would be attending who did not already know Alessandra well, Ursula dressed and coiffed her with the greatest care. She had a gown made out of the blue silk with its crop of seed pearls. The heavy garment felt more like a shroud than a wedding dress to Alessandra when she tried it on.

Ursula spent hours weaving matching blue silk ribbons into Alessandra's hair. It was a bittersweet feeling for her, as she couldn't remember ever having been touched by Ursula with such tenderness or at such great length. Ursula chatted gaily about the banquet and the various delicacies she'd instructed Cook to prepare: roast suckling pig with figs and cinnamon, sausage-stuffed capons, and brandied eels.

She even praised Alessandra when the last ribbon was tied. "You look a perfect picture, *cara!* Worthy of"—Ursula paused meaningfully—"a very rich gentleman indeed!"

Alessandra's papa had assured her that Ursula was still searching for a son-in-law worthy of her ambitions. "If so, Madame, then this is a sight I'd like to see. May I look in my Lady's mirror?"

"Oh, Zan-Zan," cooed Ursula—and truly the nickname sounded loathsome coming from her, as if it had been spoken by a snake. "Won't you ever call me 'Mother'?"

Alessandra wanted to say "Never!" But she held her tongue and peered silently into the circle of polished bronze Ursula held before her.

There was something new about her face she hadn't seen the last time, perhaps a year ago, that she'd looked into her mother's mirror—for it was her mother's mirror, or had been. The bones of her face seemed better defined than before. She reached up and touched the bone beneath her cheek, the softer bone of her nose—was it bone, or something else? Skulls always had only a hole there.

"You're a lovely young woman now—a fruit that's nearly ripe for plucking. A year in the convent, and then there will not be a virgin in Emilia-Romagna who will command a higher bride-price—or merit a grander bridegroom!" Ursula reached out and pinched both of Alessandra's cheeks hard enough to hurt. "There!" she said, without a hint of cruelty in her voice.

Like a pig, thought Alessandra, *being primped and fattened and brought to market.*

The bells rang for Sext, twelve peals through the golden, sun-flecked, midday air. "To the window, Alessandra!" Ursula was half pulling and half pushing her to the largest window, which faced out over the square. "Just so, dear—no, lean on the sill a bit. More to the middle—hurry!"

The sun was warm on Alessandra's cheeks, which were still smarting from being pinched. She heard the sound of horse's hooves clattering on the cobblestones below.

"Don't move!" said Ursula before stepping back from the window, but not so far back that she couldn't see out into the square.

Two riders approached at a pretentious gallop—one a gentleman and the other evidently his servant. They pulled up short beneath the window. The gentleman removed his hat and bowed. He was a man about her father's age, and someone Alessandra had never seen before. She kept her face composed, only nodding ever so slightly to answer his bow. And then, leaving a wake of dust shot through with sunlight behind them, the riders galloped away in the direction of Bologna.

Nicco, just coming back from the stables, saw the whole thing and was left brushing the other riders' dust off his clothes.

"Who's that old git, then?" he called up to Alessandra.

Alessandra, keeping her gaze facing outside, away from Ursula, looked down at Nicco and crossed her eyes.

Nicco wiped the smile off his face when Ursula appeared side by side with Alessandra in the window. He noticed how his sister had grown—perhaps from all that time spent lying in bed: She was just a hand's breadth shorter than Ursula now.

"That, young Niccolò," Ursula said magisterially, "is a very wealthy man, owner of two castles and vast tracts of land in a delightfully distant province."

Alessandra turned to her. "May I take this dress off now, Madame?"

Ursula, dismissing Alessandra with a wave of her hand, continued to look out the window.

Nicco called up to her, "You're not planning to give our Alessandra to him?"

"I would, readily enough, but the gentleman already has a wife." Ursula laughed—a thing she did rarely enough. "No, we have promised Alessandra to his only son. Your father has gone to a great deal of trouble over the matter—far more trouble, in my opinion, than was deserved."

Eight

That summer went by quickly for Alessandra, filled as it was with her observations of all that she was about to leave behind. She wanted to spend more time with her siblings than they seemed to have for her suddenly, as if they'd simply accepted the idea that she was leaving for the cloister, and had replaced her already in their hearts and habits.

She couldn't help but notice and feel hurt by Ursula's uncharacteristic good cheer, evidently at the prospect of getting rid of her least favorite stepchild. Alessandra looked, as always, to her father's library for comfort—

and wondered if books and learning were to be her sole lifelong companions.

There were two aspects of her plan that especially troubled her, driving her to steal into Ursula's room and look into the polished bronze of her mother's mirror whenever she could do so undetected.

Alessandra's mother had been a person of celebrated beauty, both inside and outside, and a model of womanhood held up all around the parish—a lady who did good works quietly, without crowing about them. Who managed to show both justice and affection to her children. Who was a helpmate to her husband but also a companion to his heart, held in the tenderest esteem by him.

The face Alessandra saw in the mirror belonged to an awkward, lonely, and frightened girl who was nonetheless filled with a sense of her own momentous destiny. Who was about to leave all safety and comfort behind her, as well as every similarity she bore to the saintly mother she loved so well.

Pierina was right: The risks applied to all of them. Shame, censure—even financial ruin, if the Church or the *Podestà* sniffed out Alessandra's deception. She'd looked in

some law books from her father's library: if she'd understood them correctly, her father could be held responsible
for every rule broken by her, every flouting of convention, every breach of the law, both civil and sacred, that
she incurred. His land, his books, and his business would
all be liable.

She cried, alone in her room, thinking of Nicco
reduced to working as a laborer on someone else's land,
and Pierina—beautiful Pierina—dowerless and relegated
to a lifetime of servitude. And her papa?

This thought made her weep hardest of all. Her papa,
who believed in her obedience and goodness as no father
had ever believed in his daughter before, with such trust
and faith and love—her papa would die of shame and sorrow if Alessandra's deception were made known.

She would have to cover her tracks so thoroughly
that not one single suspicion would be raised, either in
her home or at the convent. But such an enterprise—
she was worldly enough to know—would require not
only determination and careful planning but also a great
amount of gold.

Alessandra put down the mirror, dried her tears, and

crossed herself. She closed her eyes and imagined her future, and could picture no other path but this one stretching out before her—however difficult and solitary. However far it led from the sort of future her loving father dearly wanted for her.

She prayed to the mother of God—and to her own mother—to understand and forgive her for what she was planning to do.

The call of a nightjar woke Alessandra from a troubled dream. All she could recollect of it was that she was lost in a strange and ominous land. The birdsong was part of the dream, but she couldn't remember how, except to recall that she felt afraid, as if something—or someone—were pursuing her.

She lay there in her bed, looking out at the shimmering glimpse of Heaven that showed through her window. And then she heard the *chirrup* again, recognizing it this time—now that she was more completely awake—as Nicco's call to her to come out into the night.

Before Ursula had begun keeping such close watch on her, Alessandra and Nicco—and, later, Pierina—had occasionally climbed up and down the ancient wisteria vine that clung to the stones of the house and perfumed Alessandra's room with its purple blossoms all through the spring and summer. Ursula found out about these nighttime jaunts and caused the vine to be cut so that it reached too far below Alessandra's window to allow her escape.

On full-moon nights, Alessandra would lie in her bed and remember the delicious feeling of being abroad in the silvery, dangerous world of the nighttime.

It was a grinning new moon now, and even the starlight was shining only faintly through the wisps of clouds that raced across the sky—not the sort of night Nicco usually chose for their rambles. Not a safe night for risking whatever evil spirits lurked in the shadows—a night that would be the darling of robbers, assassins, and demons.

Alessandra wrapped the blanket around her shoulders but shivered anyway—half from fear, half from cold. The *chirrup* might have been a nightjar, after all. She lit the candle from the banked embers of her fire, pulled on her clothes, and looked outside.

There were scant leaves left on the wisteria now, and

a few of these—she saw, with a start, when she saw his face in the window—were stuck in Nicco's hair.

"Are you going deaf?"

"I was asleep!" She held her hand out to him. He grasped it and pulled himself up far enough to crawl through the window.

"I have something for you, Zan—and I'm going to ask for something in return." He stared at her, his blue eyes snapping in the firelight. "Talk!"

Alessandra looked with determination out the window and into the darkness. She longed to tell Nicco everything—and to ask his advice. But she only shook her head. "I leave for the cloister in three months' time. What would you have me say?"

He stood close to her, waiting until she met his eyes. "To the others—to our stepmother, lie all you want, although you put your soul in mortal peril. But do not lie to me, Alessandra!"

"Then do not ask me questions!"

"I know you're planning something—and Pierina knows it, too. Damn it, why won't you let us help you?"

She whispered her reply. "It's something that I can

only do alone." She took both his hands in hers, and felt how dear they were to her—and how much it would cost her never to hold them again.

"Just tell me this—you're going to live with the Sisters of Sant'Alba—just nod, yes or no."

In the firelight, Alessandra nodded once, very slowly.

"And you will marry, in one year's time, the person our father has chosen for you?"

"Ah, don't ask me that!" Alessandra knelt and stirred the fire and put some more wood on it. Her face looked golden in the circle of light.

"You will take the veil?" Nicco hazarded.

Without looking at him, Alessandra shook her head no.

"Have you fallen in love with someone else?"

"How could I, Nic, unless he were a phantom? I'm allowed to see no one, and no one sees me!"

Nicco took her by both shoulders. They felt far too delicate and girlish to contend with the dangers of the world.

"Whatever you're planning," he said, "you might have need of this. . . ." He took his dagger out of its scabbard— the dagger he carried with him everywhere, which he used to kill animals and cut them apart, to spear his food at table, and to defend himself from predators, assassins, and thieves if he was caught on the road after dark. "You'll need to know how to use it, and how to keep it razor sharp."

She reached up and touched his cheek, where a beard—though fine and light colored—had begun to grow. "But your knife! Surely you need it yourself."

"I'll tell Father that it was wrested from me in a game of chance. Or, better yet, lifted from me by a whore."

"Oh, Nic!"

"Such a tale would please him. He'll wink and then buy me another knife." Nicco unbuckled the scabbard and gave that to Alessandra, too.

She held both objects in her hands, put the knife in its sheath, and embraced her brother.

"And this, too," he said, pushing her away and placing a heavy little leather bag in her hands. "It's not very much, but it's all I have." She could see the glint of tears in his eyes, and how he blinked to make them go away. "Just promise me, Alessandra, that you'll call out to me for help if you need it! There is no risk I would not take for you."

"You are the best of brothers!"

She opened the bag and counted out the ten coins it held. "How long, would you say, a man could live on this amount of money?"

Nicco looked at her slantwise. "Here—or in some city?"

"In some city," said Alessandra.

"A year, I'd say, if that man lived carefully."

She kissed his hands. "Thank you, Nic!"

"You won't tell me more?"

She looked into his brave, blue eyes. "I'll send word to you from the convent."

Her promise clearly made him happy. "Here, Zan," he said, taking the knife from her. "I'll show you how to make it sharp enough to slice through flesh as if it were butter." He brought a sharpening stone out of his pocket and spat on it.

Nicco's knife—even Alessandra couldn't guess that night how important a tool it would prove to be for her. How it would, in a sense, determine the course of her entire future.

❖   ❖   ❖

The family was gathered around the hearth. Alessandra was teaching Dodo his letters, incising them one by one into the skin of an apple with her little penknife—a gift from her father that doubled the number of knives she suddenly owned. If Dodo named the letter correctly, she let him take a bite of the apple. When every surface of the apple was incised and eaten, Dodo was allowed to feed the core to Nicco's dog, and they started on another apple.

The sun had set. The day itself had been overcast, and there wasn't enough light now, of course, for reading. Pierina and Giorgio sang, though softly, as Ursula complained of a headache. Nicco sat and sharpened the new hunting knife his father had bought for him, as predicted, to replace the one he gave to Alessandra. She'd taken to wearing the dagger, well hidden, under her gown. He watched his sister as she carved each letter, the tip of her tongue in the corner of her mouth.

Carlo, walking in from outside, looked over his elder daughter's shoulder. "Hearken to this, Giorgio," he said. "I think I'll fire you and hire Alessandra in your stead. She draws letters with her penknife that rival those you make with your finest brushes."

Both Giorgio and Pierina joined him to look over Alessandra's shoulder.

"What a waste," said Pierina, "to have something so beautiful merely eaten! Dodo doesn't give a fig what the letters look like."

"*Effe!*" said Dodo, barely waiting till Alessandra told him he was right before pulling the apple to his bright strong teeth and taking a big bite where the *F* had been.

"I taught you in just the same way," said Emilia.

Ursula spoke from her place closest to the fire. "How came you to read? Wasn't your father—what was it? An ostler?"

"He did indeed, *Signora*, look after the Bishop's horses. And the Bishop himself taught me my letters, although with a slate rather than an apple. My brother and me would practice our letters on afternoons when we worked in the Bishop's orchards."

"Wasting the Bishop's good apples, no doubt," said Ursula.

Giorgio was grinning.

"Go on, then!" Pierina said to him. "Say whatever it

is you want to say, or sing it—for I would love a good laugh just now."

Giorgio used the tune of the round they were just singing to make his joke, which involved a play on the Latin word—*malum*—that means both "apple" and "evil."

"And what's the joke?" asked Ursula.

Both Pierina and Alessandra tittered, while Giorgio blushed at having shamed his mistress.

Carlo saved the day by coming closer to his wife and kissing her hand. "We have good news from the convent."

Alessandra froze.

"You *are* taking the veil!" cried Pierina reproachfully.

"Not the veil, my pet," said Ursula, poking at the fire so that the flames leapt up and lit all their faces, for a brief moment, as brightly as if it were day.

"A year of retreat," said Carlo.

Pierina tried to read Alessandra's face, but the light was once again dim and imperfect.

"Perhaps two years, or even more," said Alessandra, although her voice was, like the flames, subdued.

"Oh, a year should be quite enough," said Ursula

brightly. "And then we'll have a wedding."

Pierina wanted to look at Giorgio, but didn't dare.

Alessandra held Dodo tightly and stared into the flames. Now that her entire life was about to be transformed— even though it was a transformation that she had hoped, prayed, and planned for—all she felt was dread.

Nicco's bag of precious coins lifted a great burden from Alessandra's heart. But she knew that no matter how carefully she lived, nor how hard she worked, it could not buy enough time for what she hoped to do.

Every night, when she could hear that everyone else was sleeping, she took the icon out from under her mattress— for she could not bear to have it far away from her now. She prayed to her mother and to the Virgin to help her find the rest of the gold she would need.

Students normally used seven years to finish the philosophy degree required for admission to the medical school. But Alessandra thought she could do it faster. She knew her capacity to work hard, and she had done much of the reading already. She wondered if she could find work to pay for her food and lodgings—and worried about how she could do that work without compromising her progress. And books! How would she ever pay for them?

Every night, when she prayed, she kissed her mother's face and asked her to shed light on the path that was, for now, still shrouded in darkness and uncertainty. And every night it seemed the golden web cast over that face shone brighter.

One night, having planted too wet a kiss, mixed with her own tears, Alessandra wiped the painting dry with the edge of her sleeve. To her horror, she saw her mother's face disappear.

Gasping at the realization of what she'd done and what she'd lost, she looked at the circle of gold where her mother's face had been. And then she brought the icon closer to the candle.

The heaviness of the thing, she'd always assumed, was in the iron frame that housed the painting. With her own heartbeat nearly audible, she rubbed more of the precious paint away—until she saw that the picture had been painted on a solid piece of gold.

❖ ❖ ❖

The day for her removal to the convent came much more quickly than Alessandra had imagined possible, as if the very nature of time itself had suddenly changed. So many of the things she'd planned to do a last time, or even for the first time—things she hoped to say and things she'd hoped for the chance to unsay—all of it burst like a soap bubble now, and there was nothing left but the cold, gray dawn of her departure.

A cart was hired to carry them all to the doors of the convent. Alessandra brought her birds with her (although she would far rather have brought some of her father's books—an impossibility, given their great value and the dangers of the road). She was made to wear the heavy, blue silk dress, covered over for the journey by a mouse-brown cloak.

While weaving the matching blue ribbons into her hair, which tumbled down to the middle of her back now, Ursula assured Alessandra that the wealthier she looked on her arrival, the better the nuns would treat her.

Emilia was to stay with her and serve her: Alessandra's father had insisted on it, and her stepmother—who disliked Emilia just as she disliked every reminder of the mistress who preceded her—exulted to thus be ridding herself of two annoyances at the same time. Alessandra, who had sewn the heavy gold wafer into the hem of her chemise, was still mulling over the question of how she was going to *deal* with Emilia now that she had, by default, become part of her plan.

Nicco was nowhere to be found when they were ready to leave. His horse was gone from the stable, and Alessandra knew it was because he didn't want to cry in front of them. She clutched the knife in its scabbard where she kept it hidden beneath her gown, and knew that her brother loved her.

Ursula was the only one who spoke at all during the journey, prattling on so gaily that even Carlo avoided meeting her eyes, looking out at the landscape instead, gray with rain. Everything smelled of damp leaves and woodsmoke. Alessandra was savoring the wide-open spaces and fresh air, despite the drizzle. She, Pierina, and Dodo huddled together under a blanket. Pierina wept softly. Dodo, who never liked waking early, lay sprawled across both of them, fast asleep.

Giorgio had said good-bye at the house. He

embraced Alessandra, and sang in his sweet, clear voice, "Godspeed!"

The journey didn't last long enough. As Carlo helped Alessandra down from the cart, he looked into her eyes and said her name. And then he whispered to her, "I hope you'll see, a year from now, the justice of the course I've chosen for you."

She bit down hard on her lip as she hugged him. "I know you've chosen out of love for me." And then, her voice trembling, she added, "Thank you, Papa, for all the love you've shown me—and for anticipating my every need!"

She tried to see if he knew what she meant. The heavy wafer of gold, heated through by her own skin, felt warm against her.

Carlo simply nodded. "Yes, I've tried—and only time will reveal if I've chosen well."

Ursula looked on, smiling while father and daughter whispered together. She felt generous in this final hour, knowing that the next morning would dawn without the irksome presence of either Alessandra or Emilia. Families were discouraged from visiting their daughters, as contact with the outside world was contrary to the purposes of the cloister.

Alessandra curtsied and kissed her stepmother's hand. Pierina jumped down from the cart and threw her arms around her sister, sobbing unreservedly.

"Come off with me for a moment," Alessandra said to her, looking at her father for permission. "Is it all right?"

Carlo nodded, and Alessandra walked off with her arm around Pierina, far enough away where they couldn't be heard. But no words passed between them. Pierina's eyes overflowed, but she sniffed and stifled her sobs. They hugged so hard then that it seemed to each of them their hearts would break. Pierina asked, "How will I remember her without you here to help me?"

Alessandra had no answer for her.

Dodo wailed when she said good-bye, kissing her wetly with his red lips, as pretty as a girl's. Emilia cried freely, torn between sorrow at leaving three of the children behind and relief that at least there would be someone to watch over absentminded Alessandra.

At last, when every embrace was given and every word

said, Carlo rang the bell and two black-clad nuns appeared. They attached themselves to Alessandra and Emilia like crows to carrion, leading them away, out of the daylight, into the cloister.

Emilia found herself with not enough to do for the first time in all her forty years.

Alessandra had little need and less desire for a lady's maid. Emilia folded and refolded the items of clothing they'd brought along, and picked sprigs of lavender from the convent garden to tuck between them. She regularly brought out and aired the blue silk dress, making sure it was safe from mold and mice. But Alessandra shooed her away when Emilia tried to brush her hair or wash her feet, saying, "I cannot think, Emilia, with you fussing about me so!"

When the day was fair, Alessandra sat in the garden to plan and dream, with a prayer book, as often as not, sitting open but unread across her lap.

It was a silent convent, at least as regarded the professed nuns—and the lack of conversation was driving poor Emilia half mad. She'd taken to talking to Alessandra's two finches, complaining about the scant food, the inferior quality of the linens, and the cold. She spoke of the advantages of marrying young and marrying well, of the silliness of girls who thought themselves unready for marriage, despite the fact that she herself was married and a mother by the age of fourteen. She entrusted to the birds all sorts of confidences she hoped Alessandra would overhear and take to heart.

But Alessandra fled whenever Emilia launched into one of her one-way dialogues with the birds. She'd find a tall narrow window that let her sit and listen to the rain. She sat in the library and explored the books there—although there were only a few, and those of little interest, that weren't to be found in her father's library at home.

A couple of the novices were friendly, but mostly the nuns kept their distance from her. Emilia was surprised to see Alessandra—normally a curious and outgoing girl—show so little interest in the other inmates of the place where they would both be spending a year or more. Emilia made up for the indifference of her young mistress by forging good relationships, first in the kitchen and then in the laundry. It exasperated her that Alessandra hardly seemed to notice how the quality of both the food and their linens had improved after such a short time, thanks to Emilia's efforts.

For all the sweetness of her nature, Alessandra could indeed be exasperating. She seemed to keep a veritable arsenal of secret objects beneath her skirts now—a notebook in which she scribbled furiously whenever she thought Emilia wasn't looking, and oddly enough, a knife—a big dagger of the very sort that Nicco had lost. Had Alessandra stolen it from him? Did the girl have some reason to fear for her safety? Emilia shook her head and held her counsel, except when she couldn't keep her thoughts to herself anymore, and spoke of her troubles to the birds.

Carlo was paying a high price to have his elder daughter cloistered among the Sisters, and they treated her

with a mixture of respect for her wealth and contempt—
or perhaps it was envy—for the worldly destiny awaiting
her.

Six months after her arrival, the Mother Superior sent a
novice to summon Alessandra. Emilia, mad with curiosity
and dread, followed along as closely as she could without
actually treading on Alessandra's heels.

The Mother Superior eyed Emilia with disapproval
before turning, rather deferentially, to the young *signorina*.
"A messenger has come with news from your home."

"Oh, Lord!" wailed Emilia. "Has that fool of a kitchen
maid burned the place down?"

"Hush, Emilia!" whispered Alessandra.

Emilia looked fearfully from the Mother Superior
to Alessandra and back again. "Not the master! Please,
Reverend Mother, tell us that the *signorina*'s father is well!"

The expression on Alessandra's face showed alarm.
"Who is the messenger, Reverend Mother, and what news
does he bring?"

The Mother Superior passed a scroll across her desk
to Alessandra.

Alessandra—who read the note holding it close to her chest, so that Emilia couldn't make out a single word of it—looked pale when she raised her eyes, but her voice was steady. "Emilia, please ready our things—only the essentials. We'll need to leave immediately."

Rising, the Mother Superior put one hand on Alessandra's head and made the sign of the cross with the other. Alessandra bowed and thanked her for her blessing before she and Emilia hurried back to their chamber.

"Bad news, Miss?"

Alessandra began assembling a small pile of her belongings. "Don't stand there staring, Emilia! Pack your things!"

"So it's only a short time we'll be away?"

"Hush and gather your belongings! We're never coming back to this place."

Emilia was trying to puzzle out what it could all mean. Then a look of happiness dawned on her face. She opened the trunk and took out Alessandra's blue silk dress, briefly touching her cheek to the pearl-studded fabric and sniffing in the scent of lavender. "It will travel so much better in the trunk, Miss." She made a quick mental inventory of their room, trying to think of some other way to carry the dress safely.

Alessandra caught her gaze. "Leave it," she said quietly.

Emilia gazed back at her, as uncomprehending as an innocent animal looking into the butcher's eyes. "But why, my pet? You'll surely need your wedding gown."

"There's no time to explain now."

Emilia reasoned that Alessandra's fiancé must be very rich indeed if such a dress were to be left behind! She placed it back into the trunk, wishing she herself were slim enough to fit into it—or that at least she could give it to one of her granddaughters. "But Pierina will want it, dear, even if you have no more need of it!"

"She can come get it then."

Slipping an escaped sprig of lavender into the silken folds, Emilia placed the dress back in the trunk. And then, furtively—as if she hoped Alessandra somehow wouldn't see her—she laid her hands on the finches' cage.

"Leave the birds, Emilia. We won't be able to carry them."

Tears leaked out of Emilia's eyes then. "We can't just leave them here, with no one to feed them! I will give them to Sister Paolina—I won't be a moment!"

Alessandra paused in her work of tying her little pile of things into a bundle. She looked at the pair of finches in their pretty cage. Their clipped wings had long ago grown back again. She wondered, even in her haste, if they would remember how to use them. "Let them go, Emilia—let them fly away." She pried the cage out of Emilia's hands, placing it on the ledge of the window— then lifted the latch of the gate. "Fly!" she whispered. She had to shake the birds out of their prison. And just as if they'd never been caged, they flew—beautifully— straight into the sky.

Fighting back her own tears, Alessandra flung the empty cage to the floor and continued her packing, not daring to meet her nanny's eyes.

It was a time of day when most of the nuns were at their work in the orchards and fields. Few saw Alessandra and Emilia leave with the comely young man who arrived on a horse and led a brindled donkey—the same that he himself had ridden two years before, when he'd arrived at their house in Persiceto.

Emilia mounted the donkey, with much drama and hoisting, sitting with her plump legs stretched out astride the saddlebags, distressed about the birds and the blue dress, and calling out to all the saints that she was about to fall off and break her noggin.

Alessandra climbed up to ride on the horse behind Giorgio. Although Emilia pelted him with questions, he was as silent as if he were one of the Sisters of Sant'Alba—and Alessandra refused to explain what in Heaven was going on.

After an hour's riding, Emilia called out, "The master's house is north, not south of here. We must turn at the crossroads. Alessandra, tell him to turn us around! Do his ears serve him as badly as his tongue?"

But Alessandra pretended not to hear, and Giorgio led them farther away and off the road completely, into a little stand of willows near a rushing stream. He and Alessandra both dismounted and suddenly, much to Emilia's horror, began stripping off their clothes.

"*Santa Maria!*" she cried. "They are possessed!"

When Alessandra had stripped down to her hose and chemise, she began putting on everything Giorgio had just taken off. Emilia watched, garment by garment, as her young mistress was transformed before her eyes from maiden to lad.

"Oh," she cried, shielding her eyes. "It is an abomination—an evil dream! *Dio mio*, let me awaken!"

Giorgio, wearing nothing but his linen breeches and chemise, tried to help Emilia off the donkey, but she kicked at him and pulled his hair. "No, you devil! You shall not have my virtue!'

Alessandra rolled her eyes. "Calm yourself, Emilia, and get down from there."

"Run, my dear girl! Save yourself! I'll hold him off as long as there's breath in my body."

Alessandra came up close to Emilia and patted her leg. "You've often said you'd do anything for me." She coaxed Emilia down to the ground. "That's the way! Now—there's a set of lovely men's clothes for you in the saddlebag."

At these words, Emilia collapsed in a quivering heap. "Let God take my soul, Sant'Agata, while I am still a virtuous woman!"

Alessandra, out of patience, stamped her foot. "What

a star-crossed moment it was when Papa thought of sending you with me! I beg you, Emilia—take off your gown and kirtle like a good girl and put on these breeches."

Emilia howled like a wounded animal.

Alessandra exchanged a look with Giorgio, who shrugged his shoulders. Turning back to Emilia, she said, "All right—don't put them on. But if you don't, I shall leave you here by yourself and the wolves will eat you as soon as darkness falls."

Emilia seemed suddenly to think better of her resistance, although she sniffed and sighed and muttered darkly about the sin of subverting one's gender, quoting chapter and verse from the Book of Deuteronomy. Alessandra stood by her, as if mistress and servant had changed roles, helping Emilia dress herself and stashing the capacious lavender- and sweat-scented everyday clothes in the newly emptied saddlebag.

Emilia's thin hair fit neatly beneath her cap. But when she looked down and saw how her much-used breasts, without the support of her kirtle, made for a convincing paunch—pooled above her belt—she shrieked in horror.

Alessandra, surveying her, looked quite satisfied. "The transformation is perfect! What do you think, Giorgio?"

Giorgio gave a nod of approval for Emilia but then shook his head at Alessandra. He touched his hair, which was cut short, in the usual style. "Y-y-y-your h-h-h—"

"My hair! You're right. Emilia, come here and put it in a braid for me."

"I won't!"

"What is the matter with you? You've been hovering around me like a mayfly for the past six months, wanting to braid my hair. Braid it now!"

"I won't let you cut off your curls, Alessandra Giliani, for I know quite well that's what you have a mind to do."

"Braid it, or I'll braid it myself—and I'm bound to make a botch of it." Alessandra got her knife out of its scabbard, now hanging from the belt at her waist. It glinted so fiercely in the noonday light and looked so long that Emilia screamed.

"You'll cut your very head off!"

"Please, Emilia—I beg you! The sun is past its zenith and we have a long way to go."

Emilia combed out Alessandra's chestnut curls, kissed

them, and then quickly wove them into a thick, ropy braid.

"Stand back now," said Alessandra. She was also a bit worried about cutting herself with the knife, which she'd sharpened often but had put to little use so far, apart from dressing game when it still belonged to Nicco. She held the braid in one hand while hacking away at it, from the neck out, with the other. She'd never cut anyone's hair before and it shocked her how tough a rope the braid was. She had to saw away at it, and despite her full intention of being brave, tears sprang into her eyes as she did so. It felt as if she was sawing off one of her own limbs.

When the last strands broke free, Alessandra looked down at this part of her that was now a separate thing. Then she handed it, half tossing it, to Emilia, who cradled it against her.

"There," said Alessandra. And then, using a voice that seemed more masculine to her—in fact, imitating Nicco, she said, "There!" again.

Giorgio smiled at her.

"You're sure you'll be all right, Giorgio? You have nearly as far to walk, I would wager, as we have to ride."

He shook his head, dismissing her concerns. "I was beset by robbers," he sang as he ripped the undergarments he wore and then smeared dirt on them, "on my way back from Bologna. They took everything—the animals, their cargo, and even my clothes."

"What conspiracy is this?" said Emilia, looking up from the precious braid, her voice brimming with outrage.

"A well-planned one, Emilio!"

"Emilio?"

"From now on, you are Emilio. Now get back up on your steed, my good man!"

Emilia let herself be pulled and pushed back onto the donkey by her cross-dressed mistress and the half-naked illuminator, all the while praying aloud, "Oh, Lord, drive the Devil from her!"

"Honestly, Emilia! I'm no more possessed than you are."

"You've a hectic flush in your cheeks." And then, when she'd taken a good look at Alessandra, she spoke in a kinder voice. "Marriage isn't that bad, whatever anyone else has told you. Not so bad as to make you run away. A wealthy gentleman, my dear! And probably too old to give you much trouble beneath your skirts, once he's managed to have his squirt and plant a seed."

Alessandra's cheeks really did flush then. "Hurry and be well, Giorgio! Not a word to anyone but the one who already knows—and to him, my affection and gratitude."

Giorgio touched his heart, waved, and then started down the road.

Alessandra called after him, "I'll send word of our address when we reach Bologna. I will never forget this—nor will my brother!"

She kicked her horse and started out in the direction of the city, with Emilia's donkey following close behind.

They could see the bristling towers of Bologna, so they knew they were getting close, and yet it seemed to take forever to arrive. Emilia was too tired and sore to even complain or ask questions anymore. Even Alessandra, who rode with ease (thanks to Nicco's instruction), was tired and aching in every part of her.

The sun was low and turning red behind them when they reached the closest northwest gate, the Porta San

Felice. The top of the Basilica glowed in the last golden rays of light. A line of birds was gathered overhead on the highest westernmost edge, unwilling to surrender the day until the sunlight disappeared. Alessandra also wanted to savor this day and this moment. She had never been to the city without one or both of her parents. *This day marks the beginning,* she told herself, *of my real life.*

The guard at the gate asked their business.

"I am a student," said Alessandra, trying to sound more like her brother than herself. She gestured with her thumb toward Emilia. "My servant."

The guard looked at them more carefully then, and Alessandra was certain that he would see through their disguises.

"Do you have lodgings?" When Alessandra, to be on the safe side, shook her head no rather than speak again, the guard stepped up close to her horse, indicating with a flick of his head that she should bend down to better hear him. "My sister and her husband let rooms to students, although they're not strictly licensed, if you know what I mean."

He flicked his head now at Emilia, as if acknowledging a

fellow of his own station. "They're clean rooms, though—no bugs in 'em. And my sister's a wicked good cook."

Both Alessandra and Emilia were hungry, and their eyes grew wide at this news.

"Can you lead us there?" Alessandra asked him.

"Well, I'm not supposed to leave the gate."

Alessandra reached into the pocket of her doublet and took out her moneybag, shaking it meaningfully.

"But seeing as there's no one else on the road but yourselves," said the guard in a predictably oily tone, "and seeing how my sister's place isn't far from here, I suppose there wouldn't be any harm—" He slipped a weathered hand out of his sleeve and held it, palm up, to Alessandra, "in showing you the way."

Alessandra dropped a silver *Bolognino grosso* in the guard's hand, which snapped closed around the coin and disappeared again.

The guard's lips parted in a smile containing more gaps than teeth. "Bologna is a confusing place, if you don't know it well, particularly after dark. This way, sir!"

Alessandra didn't dare look at Emilia, terrified she'd burst out giggling. "This way, sir!" he'd said. Soon, soon, she told her aching bones, they'd stable the animals, eat a good meal, and get to lie down. It would be Heaven, bugs or no bugs.

They went down a street overarched on both sides with porticoes.

"Everyone wants to rent out rooms to students these days," the guard went on. "Because if they do it, they're allowed to build their place out a little bit more, over the street. All the merchants are keen to do it, God knows, the greedy buggers. It's become the arsehole of the world here, so built out that the sun don't shine on the streets no more."

So this is how men spoke when they were among themselves! Alessandra saw Emilia, discreetly but distinctly, make the sign of the cross.

"Here we are then, my dear good sir!"

Alessandra wondered if she had given him too big a coin.

"Isabella! Isabella, you old slut, look what baby brother has brought for you!"

A small, brown, leathery woman who hardly seemed human came to the door, holding a candle up to their faces. Alessandra just caught the guard, out of the corner of her eye, rubbing his fingers together in a silent message to his sister—if she was his sister.

She, in turn, bellowed for someone named Tonio. A surly, none-too-clean-looking boy, about Alessandra's age, came down the stairs. "Take the horse and donkey to the stable!"

Alessandra dismounted, trying not to wince, and then started to unbuckle the saddlebags.

Emilia slipped off the donkey and stumbled up beside her. "I'll do that, sir," she said without skipping a beat, even lowering her voice, if Alessandra wasn't mistaken.

"Thank you, Emilio!" She could have kissed Emilia just then, but of course she didn't dare.

There were two other students lodging at Signora Isabella's—one studying law and the other, like Alessandra, aspiring to gain admission to the medical school. Both were clerics, with their heads shaven in the tonsure, which made it hard to tell their age. They were, in any case, far older than Alessandra. They looked at her and Emilia with a great deal of curiosity. But Alessandra parried their questions with protestations of fatigue. She and Emilia ate and retired to their room as quickly as possible.

There was a small bed for Alessandra and an even smaller one for Emilia, nothing more than a pallet on the floor. Despite her exhaustion, Emilia kissed Alessandra good night and tucked her in—and the sight of it would have amused anyone who saw them. But they were, as far as they knew, unobserved, and they fell asleep immediately.

The Porta Nova—one of the twelve gates of the city, close by Alessandra and Emilia's port of entry into Bologna—turned out to be the very place where the medical students gathered. This intelligence came to Alessandra at breakfast, over the bowl of hot milk and the hard roll that came as part of the cost of the room. She asked the other aspiring *medico*, whose name was Paolo, if he could show her where and how to enroll at the University.

Paolo snorted and said there was no need. All she had to do was pay her dues to the students' association and start attending lectures.

Books, the two clerics told her, were the biggest problem. There were always several people in line to read every book kept under lock and key in its carrel in the library or chained to its stand at the stationer's. People weren't shy about pushing and shoving, either, nor were they above taking and giving bribes for the privilege of sitting at the writing desk and making one's own copy. *Pecie*—the official copies of books rented out in pieces— were hard to come by. Paolo boasted that he was main- taining a flirtation with the stationer's daughter, who sometimes smuggled parts of books to him under her chemise. Alessandra nearly choked on her crescent roll at this piece of information.

"I'll introduce you to her, if you like," said the gener- ous Paolo. "She's such a flirt that one man more is always welcome to ogle her boobies. Although," he added, eyeing Alessandra, "you can hardly be called a man!"

She froze.

Paolo smiled at her, showing his rotten teeth. She wondered whether his tonsure was really a tonsure or only the natural retreat of the hair he once had. Also about how ugly the stationer's daughter must be to want to flirt with the likes of him. She could hardly breathe. Of course he'd seen right through her!

"Why, your voice hasn't even changed yet! How old are you, Sandro? Thirteen? Fourteen?"

Alessandra blinked a few times, taking this in. She said in a confidential tone of voice, "You won't tell anyone, will you?"

Paolo thumped her on the back, so that the bite of roll she had just taken came flying out of her mouth. She was about to apologize to the people sitting across the table from her—a merchant and either his daughter or his very young wife—until she realized that they were both too drunk to notice.

"You can depend on me!" said Paolo. "I'll wager you must be a prodigious scholar to have been sent here by your parents to study"—he lowered his voice to a mal-odorous whisper—"at such a tender age."

"I've read—rather a lot. I was also—on intimate terms, in my parish, with the stationer's daughter."

"By God!" Paolo slapped his thigh. "Boy or man, you're my sort, you are! A fellow who knows how to get on in the world. This, for instance," he said, laying a finger on the fringe of hair around his bald head, "and this," taking a fistful of his black clerical robe. "God calls us to Him not only to serve but also to survive! It was this or the army for me—and I have a powerful dislike of blood."

"You've made a strange choice of profession, then," said Alessandra, barely able to keep herself from laughing.

Paolo slumped in his chair, like a boat that's suddenly lost its wind. "It's true, it's true! But I have an even greater aversion to legal texts." He looked utterly miserable. "The truth is," he whispered, leaning close again, "I can hardly read."

"Then why are you here? There are many choices for a man, apart from priest, lawyer, or *medico*." Alessandra thought, as she said this, that the same was not at all true for her own gender. What could one be but a nun or a wife? Widows often could and did take on the work of their husband. But no woman could set out to be anything—except, perhaps, a servant.

"I ask myself that same question, all the time! Why am I here? All these bits of books piling up in my room now, and I can hardly read them. You can't know how it bedevils me! It takes me three times as long to parse out a text as the other fellows. And by the time I get to the end, I've forgotten the beginning. Half the time the letters dance around and change places and convey another meaning entirely." He groaned. "I've failed my first-year exams three times now!"

Alessandra was about to say "There, there!" and offer comfort—but stopped herself just in time, remembering that men didn't do this. She tried to think of what Nicco would say. "Bloody hell, Paolo!"

He looked at her, his eyes brimming with gratitude. "That's what I say, Sandro, old friend. Bloody hell!"

"Bloody hell!" echoed the merchant across the table from them.

The servant boy, Tonio, had come in to clear the tables. Alessandra saw the other boarders hasten to pocket whatever hard rolls were left before Tonio took them away.

As he passed her, he bent close to her ear and whispered, "Meet me at the privy, then."

At the privy? She wished Nicco were there to tell her whether that was something men did, too. She looked at Tonio, hoping to catch some clue from his expression. Then he winked at her. Alessandra hesitated, then winked back at him.

In her room, she held her head in her hands and moaned. She had no idea what anything meant anymore! Emilia, utterly worn out from the previous day's journey, was still sleeping. Alessandra put a roll in Emilia's hand, took a deep breath, then left to go out into the city, determined, beyond anything, not to go anywhere near the privy in Signora Isabella's boardinghouse.

Ten

Alessandra—now "Sandro" to her fellow students—found out a good deal during her first days in Bologna. The principal lectures were all given in the morning at locations decided on the spur of the moment by the students, who were completely in charge of the hiring and firing of masters. Lectures were held wherever a space could be found, depending on the weather and the master's willingness to let the students gather at his home, if he had one. A few of the most highly revered masters were able to afford to rent a second house especially for this purpose—among them, Alessandra learned, was the renowned and well-respected professor of medicine, Mondino de' Liuzzi, who was the very reason she'd wanted so much to study in Bologna.

She was waiting for one such lecture to start—this one out in the square, as the *magister* had earned his degree in philosophy only the year before and was teaching to support the continuation of his studies. Alessandra's ears pricked up at the mention of a woman doctor at the University of Paris.

"Oh, she's history!" said a fat youth with pockmarked skin. "Haven't you heard? She's been restrained from ever practicing again."

"Did they burn her?" someone else asked.

"No," sighed the fat youth, sounding bored. "Only banished her."

Alessandra felt more conscious than ever of her disguise. She seated herself in the middle of the throng of students attending the lecture, avoiding people's eyes and taking notes furiously. Before the end of the lecture, she'd used up her little bottle of ink, but she didn't dare ask to borrow ink from someone else. She had to simply try—in among the whispered gossip, occasional snores, and bawdy jokes of the other students—to memorize every word.

She was both exhausted and elated when she found her way back to Signora Isabella's, hoping she was on time for the midday meal. She had taken wrong turns twice, had to push her way through a throng of people gathered to watch a group of mummers, and just nearly missed being bitten by a savage dog. She was two steps up the staircase when someone grabbed her cloak, jerking her backward and pulling her into the alcove under the stairs, one hand—a filthy-tasting hand—held over her mouth. She knew even before her eyes had adjusted to the dark: It was the serving boy, Tonio.

When Giorgio got back to Persiceto, traveling the long way on foot, he really did look as though he'd been beset by robbers. He was limping, bleeding, sunburned, and cold by the time he arrived, long after dark. The kitchen maid, when she saw him, shrieked in a most gratifying way. Everyone else reacted just as Nicco had imagined they would—except Pierina. Pierina, now thirteen and growing fast, threw her arms around Giorgio, covering him in tears and kisses.

Ursula, who had been busy ministering to Giorgio's injuries when Pierina burst into the kitchen, looked from one to the other and then at her husband. He shook his head as if to indicate *I had no idea!* Giorgio started to speak, but his words were caught in a hopeless stammer and he merely blushed.

Realizing that she'd revealed what she shouldn't have, Pierina stood alongside him in an agony of embarrassment.

Carlo said, "First things first. What happened to you, lad?"

Giorgio looked like the most miserable and unwilling chorister who ever lived. "Robbers," he sang, "along the road."

Pierina fainted.

"For goodness' sakes!" said Ursula. "This house is beginning to resemble a hospital. Get water for her!" she told the kitchen maid. "And stop that mewling! You're only making things worse."

Giorgio, for all his fatigue, had adroitly caught Pierina before she hit the ground.

"The horse and the donkey?" asked Carlo. "The manuscript?"

Giorgio shook his head above Pierina's prostrate form. It was unclear whether his distress was in reference to his master's loss of property or to Pierina's public revelation of her feelings for him.

It was clear to Nicco—and, really, to all of them—that the love between these two was formidable. He could see his father entertaining the idea of a match between his best artist and his second daughter—and how his initial reaction of annoyance was replaced by the realization that nothing, in fact, could be more perfect.

Giorgio's work was a source of plenty for the family, bringing in spectacular new commissions. His reputation in the book trade was quickly growing. Carlo had been gnawed by fear that one of the rich private collectors in the region—perhaps Romeo Pepoli himself—would try to lure Giorgio away. The Giliani workshop could never come up with that sort of gold. But what girl in the parish was more charming than Pierina, with her blond hair, blue eyes, and winning ways? To have such an artist as his son-in-law—that would be the greatest triumph of all.

Nicco also liked the idea. He already loved Giorgio like a brother. And this would mean that Pierina—unlike Alessandra—would stay at home.

Ursula, secure in the knowledge that her elder step-daughter would command a high bride-price, seemed to find no fault with the idea of a humbler match for Pierina. She was glad, too, that her favorite stepchild would remain close by. Ursula merely looked at her and murmured, "So young!"

By the time Pierina woke from her swoon, with very little being said, she found herself betrothed to the young man she'd loved since first laying eyes on him.

Realizing it was Tonio—and not someone older or even much stronger than she, judging by his size—Alessandra grabbed the hilt of her knife, hoping dearly she wouldn't have to use it. Tonio took note and let go of her after getting her assurance in pantomime that she wouldn't cry out.

She spat, then wiped her mouth. "What do you want, you blackguard?"

Tonio laughed. Underneath the dirt, Alessandra saw,

he was barely more than a child. The serrated edges of his new adult teeth had not yet been worn smooth. He, like she, still had all his teeth—which was perhaps the only luck this boy had ever known. She wondered in what cowshed in what mean village he'd been brought into the world—and how he came to be the servant at Signora Isabella's.

"'Blackguard'! That's a fancy word!"

"You rodent then—you flea!"

"I've been called worse in my time."

"You seem proud of it."

"A man takes what opportunities as he can to feel a sense of satisfaction."

"As if you were a man!"

"As if *you* were!"

Alessandra readjusted her cloak. Under Tonio's persistent stare, she reached down and grabbed the crotch of her breeches, shifting the fabric there as she'd seen her brother and his friends do when standing around the square together. "State your business, flea! I want my dinner."

"Well, I want my money!"

"What money?"

"For my silence!" Tonio was looking at her as if convinced that she was simpleminded. "I know your secret!" he said in an exaggerated whisper.

"Do you?" Alessandra did her best to scowl at him. She pulled her cloak aside so that he could see her right hand on the hilt of her knife again.

"I won't tell," said Tonio, "not if you pay me proper!"

Alessandra pulled the knife out of its hilt and held the point under Tonio's chin. "Don't move," she said. "It's very, very sharp."

"Don't cut me, master!"

"Don't threaten me, then."

"It's only that I know—"

"You know what?"

Tonio swallowed hard. "That you're traveling with your nanny."

Alessandra lowered the knife without even meaning to. "How did you find out?"

"I saw her—well, I don't want to say it, seeing as she's old. I saw her . . ." He cupped his hands over his chest and then, thinking better of it, lowered them down to his belly, "when she was getting dressed. And last night I saw her kiss you g' night." Tonio looked wistful. Alessandra was fairly certain he had never had anyone kiss him good night.

She looked at him as if with a new sense of respect (even though all she felt was pity for him). "You're a smart lad."

"Look—just because I'm poor and you're rich, it doesn't make you any older than me, right?"

Alessandra tried to think, once again, what Nicco might do in the situation. "Mind your place!" she said. And then, throwing an arm around Tonio and speaking low into one of his dirty ears, she added, "It's true enough—she couldn't bear to be parted from me. She suckled me as a baby and she'd continue to do so, if she had her way."

"Women!" said Tonio.

"They're all the same." Alessandra gave Tonio a friendly slap on the back and then hoisted up her breeches. "I told her no one would buy that disguise of hers. You won't let on, though, will you?" She got her little moneybag out and found a coin in it—a small copper one—and gave it to

Tonio. "It would hurt her something terrible."

"Seeing as how you've put it so persuasive-like . . ." Tonio smiled with satisfaction at the expensive word that came to him, as sweet and miraculous as the honey the bees pulled out of the air.

Alessandra tried to hide the sigh of relief that escaped her. "I'm glad to know I can trust you. There may be things that will come up, things that—" She jerked her head toward the room she shared with Emilia and said softly, "—she or I might need done."

"I'm your man, Sandro." A look of anxiety passed over Tonio's features. "Is it all right to address you so?"

"When it's just the two of us, you may use my Christian name."

Alessandra knew that she had an ally now at Signora Isabella's—and thanked her lucky stars she had an older brother.

"Papa," said Pierina a few weeks after her betrothal. "Dearest Papa!"

"I quake with fear when I hear those words," said Carlo.

"Sweetest Papa!"

Carlo held up his hands as if to ward off a blow.

"Darling Papa!"

"Slay me now, Pierina, and have done with it!"

She kissed him on the cheek and scooted close enough to rest her head on his shoulder. "You know I can't marry until after Alessandra has her wedding."

"What of it?"

She laced her arm through his. "Can't she be persuaded to have it sooner?"

Carlo put a bit of space between them. "Are you in such a hurry, my poppet?" He looked more closely at her, examining her luminous skin and clear blue eyes. "You're not—"

"No," said Pierina, perhaps a little too quickly. "But I want to start my married life without delay."

"You have time!"

"Who knows how much time any of us has on this Earth? And you know how Alessandra is—she will put off her marriage as long as she can, because . . ." Pierina looked a little guilty. "Because she doesn't love her fiancé, does she? Not like I love my Giorgio!"

"Alessandra has not met her fiancé, Pierina."

"And you shouldn't let her meet him, either—not till the wedding! She's bound to find some objection to him, despite the brilliant match you've made for her." She lowered her voice. "You do not know my sister like I do, Papa! She is unnaturally stubborn."

"Whereas you are docile and obedient?"

"I would be, forever and ever, if you hurried things up a bit. We could even have the weddings on the same day—wouldn't that be lovely?" Pierina looked very pleased with herself. "We could have one big feast instead of two."

Carlo spoke sternly. "You seem to forget your place, Pierina, as my second daughter."

"Oh, I haven't at all, Papa! I know that Alessandra's betrothal is the only reason why Mother has agreed to let me marry Giorgio, besides wanting to keep me close by. One brilliant marriage is, after all, as much as any family needs."

Unlike her big sister, Pierina had no gift for seeing when she was being teased—and always rose to the bait.

Carlo assumed his most thoughtful expression, as if

he were suddenly reconsidering everything. "So," he said slowly, "if Alessandra does not marry the man I've chosen for her, then you will agree to make a brilliant marriage for us instead?"

Pierina pushed away and stamped her foot. "How you vex me, Papa!"

Her show of pique banished Carlo's playful mood. "You will do as I say, daughter!"

Pierina knelt before him. "I must marry Giorgio! A fortune-teller told me I would marry a dark-eyed man from Padova."

"There are many men who fit that description, and from far more illustrious families, who could probably be convinced to take you as a wife."

"Please, Papa! Alessandra will be happy enough, once she gets used to the idea."

"And do you not think that your sister deserves the sort of happiness you feel?"

"Oh, Alessandra does not even know what it means to love someone. All she cares about is Aristotle."

"To love someone." As Carlo repeated his daughter's words, a shadow passed over his features. "Well, my child,

I am glad that you, at your tender age, have pondered so deeply the ways of Earth and Heaven, and understand them better than your sister—and perhaps better than everyone else in this household."

Pierina looked at him fearfully. "Can't Nicco make a brilliant marriage," she asked in a small, chastened voice, "if Alessandra won't?"

"Enough!"

"Forgive me, Papa!"

"Go to your room! Ask God for His forgiveness, and to mend your spoiled ways."

Eleven

On Saturday morning, the crier passed by Signora Isabella's, announcing that the water at the neighborhood bathhouse was good and hot.

"Quick, Emilia!" said Alessandra, shaking her awake. "Change into your gown! We must go bathe today—I feel I will die if I don't."

Alessandra had already pulled on the chemise, gown, and kirtle that had lain folded and hidden away.

"I will, with pleasure, Mistress! But how will we leave this house without being seen?"

"Just dress yourself! We'll look out in the hallway and pass quickly. And if anyone sees us, perhaps they'll take us for a couple of whores ordered up by our other selves."

"Oh, the whole thing makes my head spin," said Emilia, who was nonetheless getting up and dressing with unaccustomed alacrity. "I can't keep track of who I am, one minute to the next."

"Well, in a very short time," whispered Alessandra as she cracked the door and gazed out into the hall, "both Emilia and Emilio will be much cleaner and more comfortable. Go now!" They darted out of the room and down the stairs, both of them giggling at the irony of disguising themselves as women.

They slowed their pace, both out of breath, as soon as they'd rounded the corner.

"How odd to be out and about in Bologna, dressed like this!"

Emilia was looking all about her, touching her gown and her unloosed hair, and looking down at her newly restored bosom, with obvious pleasure. "Do you really think they'd stop you from going to lectures if you showed up as yourself?"

"I don't want to risk it. I haven't seen a single other female student."

They knew they'd reached the bathhouse by the cloud of steam coming from the windows. "This will be a treat for me, Emilia—far more hot water, I'll wager, than in the laundry tub you bathed me in at home."

Alessandra paid their entry and bought soap for them. They passed by some private curtained rooms, where servants waited on the couples within—illicit lovers, all of them, who could only meet in secret, away from their homes. Emilia sighed at the thought of all the wickedness in the world. "Maybe it's not such a bad thing for you, after all, to hide yourself, out as you are among all those men and their wanton desires."

"Yes," said Alessandra as she pulled off her clothes. "The only feeling Sandro inspires among them is rivalry." She lowered herself into the water. "Oh, Emilia—I've died and gone to Heaven!"

Alessandra tried to be as inconspicuous as possible during lectures. But when she knew a subject well, she would approach the professor afterwards and arrange to be examined. In this way, all within the space of her first nine months in Bologna, she passed her first year's exams, then the second year's, followed by the third.

The fame of this brilliant and mysterious young man spread quickly, as did all news in the student quarter. People were calling him another Abelard. All sorts of stories sprang up about where he came from. He was, by some accounts, an Arabian prince traveling with his eunuch. There was another rumor that made the young man a nephew of the King of Burgundy. The story that was soonest quashed said that this Sandro was actually a girl from a wealthy family, traveling with her nanny, both of them dressed in men's garb. No one believed that one, and it was soon dismissed as altogether implausible.

Alessandra withdrew more and more frequently into the sanctuary of the seven churches of Santo Stefano, to ask forgiveness for the sinful pride she took in her accomplishment, as well as for the sin of disguising her gender. She confessed once a week to the oldest, most wizened priest she could find, and made sure he saw the coins she put in the offertory. To her great comfort, he seemed every week to have forgotten everything she'd confessed to him the week before. She took Communion from him and hoped he wouldn't give her away.

In the dappled light and shadows of the innermost sanctuary of Santo Sepolcro, she knelt on the cold stone to pray for the courage to carry on. She prayed to her mother to intercede for her, to plead her case and send her the strength and determination that she knew she needed every waking hour.

Sometimes she stayed there until her knees had no sensation, too confused and afraid to step out into the light again. Why would God have given her a keen and questioning mind if He didn't intend her to use it? Why would the world and all of Nature be laid out like a book, waiting to be read and understood, if the Creator had not desired her to discover its secrets and draw wisdom from them? Wasn't it a sign of respect to try to better the lot of the creatures God had favored above all others with intelligence and reason?

Woman was created last of all, after all the animals and after Adam himself. Why would God have done it thus if He intended woman as a lesser creature? Would He not then have made her just after the animals and before Adam?

Alessandra sat there in the twilight of the church, surrounded by the entombed spirits of the dead. She knew she would have to oppose all the powers on Earth to accomplish what God had given her the ability and ambition to do.

Alessandra was sitting among the throng of scholars at a lecture by Mondino, taking careful notes on everything he said and jotting down questions she hoped to ask him later. Halfway through, she turned around, aware of someone's attention trained on her rather than on the eminent doctor. She felt it as surely as if an insect had been hovering around her head—and she wished that, whoever he was, she could as readily swat him away.

He sat behind her and a little bit to the side. He was handsome and well made for that bookish crowd, and he wore the clothes of a gentleman, although carelessly, as if his wealth was of little concern to him. His eyes were dark and yet full of light. He met and held Alessandra's eyes, which flashed at first with annoyance and then softened. She took in the rich binding of his notebook, his chiseled profile, and his beautiful hands—

and then she turned to her own notes again.

Her heart was beating fast. What business did he have, looking at a fellow student so intensely?

Even though the lecture was one that Alessandra had been greatly looking forward to hearing, she found herself having trouble concentrating on the rest of it. And when it was over, she resolved to wait until the following week to speak to Mondino.

Her hands felt cold while she corked her ink bottle and put her pen in its case, and yet the sun was shining and there wasn't a cloud in the cerulean sky. She stole another look over her shoulder; there were those eyes again—and this time it seemed they were laughing at her.

She swept her things into her satchel, gave him a withering look—the sort of look she imagined Nicco would give to any fellow who dared to stare at him so impertinently—and walked away with more swagger than she usually affected, trying especially hard to look both taller and older.

She thought of him, though, during the whole of her walk back to Signora Isabella's. Of all the scholars who'd come to her father's scriptorium—of all the traders passing through Persiceto, and of all the people in the town—she'd never seen any person before whose face and mien pressed themselves as precisely into her memory, as if he had been an engraved seal and she a melted pool of wax.

She hurried away as if fleeing the sweet laughter in those brown, expressive eyes, wondering if she would ever see him again and knowing that she shouldn't.

Intimate friendship would not be on Sandro's path—how could it be? Anyone who drew too close to her was bound to discover her secret.

That evening, sticking her head out the window of her room for a look at the full moon and a bit of fresh air, she saw him—at least, it looked like him—on the street below, standing as still as a statue. Whoever it was bowed and evanesced into the shadows. But the incident was alarming enough for Alessandra to resolve to find new lodgings.

When Nicco came to look for Sandro at Signora Isabella's, he was told that the young gentleman and his servant had left Bologna, called away on urgent family business.

This bit of news left Nicco scratching his head.

In fact, Alessandra had sent a note to her brother, informing him that she was seeking out new lodgings and he shouldn't send any correspondence until she could tell him precisely where. But the messenger and Nicco had passed each other on the road.

Nicco wandered rather helplessly around the student quarter. Everyone he asked, it seemed, had heard of the academic prodigy named Sandro. But no one had the slightest idea how to find him.

The rumor of Nicco's quest grew its own wings, with a proliferation of adornments. Nicco was an agent of the King of Burgundy . . . a secret assassin . . . Sandro's homosexual lover . . . Sandro's brother . . . Sandro's creditor . . . and (best of all) Sandro's unbelievably homely sister, who had donned male garb to come search for him.

Tonio, always keen to follow the scent of money, found Nicco at a tavern, waiting for the joint of meat roasting on the spit there.

"'Scuse me, Your Honor," said Tonio, simultaneously bowing and wiping his nose. It was a bad season for colds that winter, with dripping noses everywhere.

The joint was taking a long time, and Nicco had drunk

quite a few bowls of hot mulled wine by then. As a result of this, as well as his sense of fatigue and discouragement, his only words to Tonio were "Go away!"

But Tonio, used to being treated as a scourge, only came closer. "Yes," he said, squinting at Nicco in the firelight, "I can see the resemblance between you—although he's not nearly as fat!"

In a trice, Nicco grabbed Tonio by the collar, until only the long, curling points of Tonio's secondhand shoes brushed against the ground. "He's not nearly as apt to lose his temper, either!"

Tonio, undaunted, looked Nicco straight in the eyes. "He's quick with that big knife of his, though."

A smile lit Nicco's face. "You know where I can find— my brother?"

Tonio, with both feet flat on the ground again, made tender readjustments to the rags that passed as his clothes. "As it happens, Your Highness," he said, "I am one of his most trusted associates."

Nicco snorted. "Where is he, then? Tell me the truth and I'll pay you well."

Tonio moved a bit away, far enough so Nicco wouldn't

be able to grab him again. "I don't exactly know. . . ." He threw his arms up in front of his face when Nicco raised his hand—but it was only to send Tonio packing.

"Leave me be, rodent, if you have no information for me!"

"That's just what he called me!"

"One of his closest associates, are you?" Nicco took another swig of his wine, found it cold, and spat it out. "Waiter!" he called.

"I said I didn't know exactly where he was—but I didn't say I have no information." Tonio sidled close to him. "I do have information. Privileged information, I might add."

"Are you still here?"

Tonio came close enough to whisper—and Nicco moved away, repelled by the odor of his words, even while hanging on their meaning. "Both he and his nanny are still in Bologna!"

"You know about Emilia, do you?"

"I do," said Tonio, sounding very well satisfied with himself (and taking Nicco's repugnance in stride). "I also know where they buy their bit of bread and cheese of an afternoon."

"Why didn't you say so?" Nicco slapped some money down on the table to pay for his wine. "Take me there, lad, without delay! You'll be able to buy yourself some decent clothes before this day is done."

Alessandra was under considerable pressure from Emilia, who was fed up with dressing as a man. Between the come-ons of whoremongers and her utter isolation from other women during the long hours when Alessandra was immersed in her studies, Emilia grew more and more despondent. She hated that smirking ragamuffin Tonio, and was convinced that Signora Isabella was the Devil's spawn. Much to Alessandra's distress, Emilia had taken to drinking in taverns during the long and lonely afternoons. She'd sometimes forget herself then, doing or saying things that might imperil the secrecy of their entire enterprise.

After a day spent inquiring after new long-term lodgings—a day she hated taking away from her studies—Alessandra realized that the only way to allow Emilia to go back to dressing like a woman was to unmask her as Sandro's nanny. There was no question of being able to start over in another part of the city as two other people; everyone, it seemed, already knew about the prodigy Sandro and his plump, womanish servant.

The reality of their situation cost Alessandra—as Sandro—in terms of her masculine pride. How could Sandro hope to be taken seriously as a scholar if he was known to be traveling in the company of his nursemaid?

They were discussing this—in truth, they were arguing about it—when Tonio brought Nicco to the threshold of their favorite bakery.

"By God," breathed Nicco as he caught sight of his sister. "She looks amazing!"

Tonio, looking at Emilia, squinted his eyes. "Do you think so? She doesn't have the figure for it at all—far too soft and lumpy."

Nicco hastened to give Tonio a silver coin. "Here, my boy! You've been wonderfully helpful."

Tonio stared at the heavy coin in his hand. It was more money than he had ever possessed in his lifetime.

"I'll give you another just like that if I find you've kept this whole thing strictly to yourself. Not a word to anyone!"

"Cut out my tongue if I tell anyone, master!"

"Now go!"

Tonio disappeared so quickly, it was as if he'd never been there.

Nicco strode inside the bakery, which was empty except for Alessandra and Emilia, who shrieked when she saw him.

"Hush!" cried both brother and sister as one.

"Are you real?" Emilia stretched out her hand to touch Nicco's cheek. "You must be real, because spirits don't have prickly whiskers—I'd swear by it!"

"Nic!" Alessandra couldn't help it: She threw her arms around her brother.

"You didn't think I wouldn't come, did you?"

"I'm so glad to see you!"

"You look thin, Alessandra. Emilia, you're here to see that she eats properly!"

Alessandra shushed him. "I'm 'Sandro' here—and I'm 'he,' not 'she,' as far as the world concerns itself with me."

"Which is quite a lot, from what I've heard—Sandro! You're the most famous student in Bologna, it would seem."

"Well, I want to stay famous, if I must be famous, for the right reason. Oh, Nic—I've missed you so!"

They clasped hands and looked into each other's eyes.

Alessandra hadn't allowed herself to feel so weak and vulnerable since her arrival in the city, nearly a year ago. It required all her self-control not to break down into tears.

Nicco looked a proper man now. She wondered if she had also changed, reached up to touch her cheek, and then laughed when she realized how very different she looked since her brother last saw her.

"Come away with me, Sis—come home!"

"Don't be daft—I can't."

"Oh, Mistress!" said Emilia, wide-eyed with excitement. "Couldn't we? I am so lonely for Persiceto and all its comforts! How is Dodo? And our Pierina?"

"Dodo can shell peas and count to one hundred. And our Pierina . . ." He turned to Alessandra. "Pierina and Giorgio are betrothed."

Alessandra stared. "Betrothed? But, Nic"—she grabbed his hands again—"Nic, she's too young!"

Emilia, beside herself with happiness, wiped her face

with the rough linen of her sleeve.

"She's so happy," said Nicco. "And it means that both of them will stay at home."

Alessandra paused, taking it all in. "It will have to be a long betrothal! Pierina can't marry until I do—and I'm going to avoid the event altogether, if I can."

Emilia surprised both of them by pointing out the obvious. "That's the most selfish thing I've ever heard you say, my pet. Would you have your sister be a spinster to suit your whims?"

"She's only thirteen, Emilia—I mean Emilio. Oh, bother! She's hardly in danger of becoming a spinster. And at the rate I'm going, I can get my degree in philosophy next year and go on to the medical school."

Both Nicco and Emilia were looking at her the way they did when she was little and they'd caught her out in a misdeed of one kind or another.

"I am studying as fast as I can, I do assure you! And I will not marry now, no matter how many castles my bridegroom owns!"

"You might like him," said Nicco. "Father took a lot of trouble about choosing him."

"Or was it our stepmother who chose him?" She sighed. "Marriage is out of the question, anyway. I have work to do!"

Emilia gave a loud and audible sigh. "Poor Pierina!"

"She can wait!"

"Your year is up, Sis—you're expected to come home from the convent this Christmas. It's been all I can do to keep any of the family from visiting you there these past twelve months. I've run out of astrological events to keep them from traveling. In fact, they think I've gone there now, to bring you home."

"Well, I won't go. How can I?"

"Oh, be reasonable, for a change, Zan! You've had your year of breaking all the rules. You've stayed alive—cut your losses, girl!"

"You think it's been merely a matter of breaking rules?" Alessandra shook her head. "You don't know me, Nic."

"I know you better than you know yourself—and I certainly know the world better than you do."

"Not at this point, you don't! I've lived on my own here and made a good job of it, too."

"On your own you've lived, have you?" asked Emilia

with a shake of her shoulders that would have fluffed out her feathers if she'd been a bird. "And I suppose I haven't devoted my days and nights to looking after you!"

Alessandra, forgetting herself altogether, gave Emilia a kiss on the cheek. "You've been wonderful, Emilia. And, truly, you should go home now. Go home with Nic!"

"But who will protect you, my little love?"

It was infuriating how, after all the strength and resourcefulness Alessandra had shown, Emilia still treated her like a child. It was her turn to sigh impatiently. "These clothes are my protection. Sandro, my alter ego, is my protection. I'm in need of no one else." Alessandra looked at both of them. "Not even you, Emilia! Go home to Persiceto. I'm sure you'll be most welcome there."

"I wonder," said Emilia.

"Father will see to it that you are. Take her home with you, Nic—please! Truly, I never meant to involve her."

Nicco looked at Emilia, who seemed to be pleading with him to agree despite her protestations—and then at his sister, who had that stubborn look she got on her face when she wouldn't be swayed from a decision, not for anything. He pushed his hair back from his forehead. "At least promise me you'll come home for Easter! I'll come get you."

"I can come by myself." She pulled her cloak aside to show Nic's old knife, always kept by her side now. "You forget—you taught me well."

"Too well, by all appearances."

"It is not out of desire to be one of your gender that I dress this way." Alessandra thought of her mother's portrait, a nipped-at piece of gold now, with only traces left of the Virgin's robe and the feet of the angel Gabriel.

She suddenly missed home. She wanted to see her other siblings and go by herself to the storage room, where she could open the trunk of her mother's clothes and touch her cheek to them. "I'll come," she said. "I promise. There will be no lectures, anyway, on the holy days at Eastertime."

Nicco held her by both forearms and smiled. "Good man, Sandro!" he said loud enough for anyone in the place to hear.

"But I will have to find new lodgings between now and then—and it is no easy thing these days, with the city overflowing with students."

"Never worry." Nicco laughed. "I know just the little man who will turn Bologna inside out to help you!"

Twelve

Under the influence of another silver coin from Nicco, Tonio asked Sandro where in all of Bologna he would most like to lodge. And Alessandra told him, "At the home of the great doctor, Mondino de' Liuzzi. I've heard that he and his wife take in boarders."

The fact that Mondino had already heard of Sandro made Tonio's job rather easy. As it happened, a room in Mondino's house had just become available, as the student occupying it had been called away on family business. Sandro could move in that very day. Tonio himself would carry Sandro's belongings and show him the way.

To Alessandro, Mondino's household was strongly and pleasantly reminiscent of her own home in Persiceto. The baby, Leoncio, was just Dodo's age, and Maxie, the elder daughter, was the same age as Pierina. Mina was Mondino's second wife—but, unlike Ursula, she loved and was beloved by all her husband's children.

The other boarder, Bene, was, like Sandro, striving for admittance to the medical school. The big-boned son of a butcher in Lombardia, Bene had astonished his entire village by learning to read and do sums at an age when other children remained as ignorant as puppies. Eventually his parish collected enough money to send him to the University of Bologna, with the condition that he return to them when he earned his advanced degree. They hoped to draw skilled artisans to their village with the presence of a licensed *medico*.

Landing this spot in Mondino's household had been an enormous coup for Bene. And then along came this Sandro—wealthy, refined in his manners, and reputed to be the most brilliant undergraduate in Bologna. Bene looked for—and found—a hundred reasons to resent and dislike Sandro, from his girlish voice to his frequent—and, to Bene's mind, affected—use of Latin.

Mondino had a bit of land he'd recently acquired in Barbiano, in the hills. The land had a house on it—a ramshackle old thing, which all the family worked on every Sunday after church to make into their summer home, where they could retreat from the heat and filth of the city, grow their own vegetables, and cultivate an orchard.

For Mondino's children, these weekly jaunts to the countryside were pure delight. They saw more of their father than they ever did at home, where he was constantly called upon to diagnose the illnesses of people who came from far away to consult with him, to cut up the bodies of people who died and pronounce on the cause of their death, or to demonstrate the wonders of the human body to students and other doctors who came from as far away as Paris to attend his anatomy demonstrations at the medical school.

In Barbiano, though, Mondino liked nothing more than building and planting and sitting at the head of the table in the makeshift dining room they set up under some ancient pear trees. At night they'd light a fire outside and hang lanterns from the trees, and Lodovico, the second son, would strum a lute and sing for them—and sometimes, if she'd had a little wine, Mina could be convinced to dance.

Alessandra soon became a favorite among all the children, who saw in her an unbelievably kind and gentle boy who cuddled the baby and always offered to help with even the most womanish chores, and yet rode and hunted as well as any of the boys. Maxie—the pretty blond daughter who reminded Alessandra so much of Pierina—Maxie grew pale and silent whenever Sandro was near, even though she always contrived to sit by him at table. She did her best to distance herself from Bene, though, whose poverty and humble origins repelled her.

Alessandra was so enjoying the respite from her cares—due to the success of her disguise in her new lodgings—that she failed to notice either that Bene hated Sandro or that poor Maxie had fallen in love with him.

Despite Mondino's reputation and the high esteem in which he was held, the cost of maintaining his large household was always just a bit more than his earnings. So when Otto Agenio Lustrolano came along, offering to pay a princely sum to rent the third extra room in the main house—a small, mean room that had been used previously for storage—his offer was gladly accepted.

Out of fairness for the price paid, Signora Mina moved Bene out of his room, which was next to Alessandra's, and into the storage room. And thus, within the space of a month of first seeing the comely young Sandro, Otto had managed to set up things so that he would be sharing a wall with him—a wonderful arrangement, Otto reasoned, for cultivating a friendship with the famously brilliant youth to whom he felt so strangely drawn. On the weekends, when they all decamped to Barbiano, he and Sandro could get to know each other even better.

Otto had never met his equal among the youths of Lustrola—and he'd never had a brother, although he'd always longed for one. He felt an odd, unsettling sense of excitement whenever Sandro was near. The thought of making him a bosom friend was unspeakably attractive to him.

Alessandra saw Otto, for the second time in her life, at

Mondino's dinner table, where she appeared late as usual, rushing from a final disputation she'd managed to squeeze into her day.

"Sandro," said Mina. "This is Signore Agenio—our newest boarder."

"Agenio," Alessandra said. She recognized the name of the primary supplier of calf- and sheepskins to her father's workshop. She looked across the table and saw the face of the handsome scholar who had been ogling her at the lecture.

He smiled more broadly at her this time than he had that day in the square. "'Otto' to everyone present."

Alessandra looked at him longer than she should have and then blushed. Out of all the places he could have chosen to board, why had he chosen this one? It was too unfair! Grabbing the last piece of bread that wasn't already sodden, she managed to say, "I'm ravenous, Signora Mina—and I'm very sorry to be late again. Is there anything left for me?"

Maxie passed Alessandra a big hunk of meat on the point of the knife she shared with her sister, Horabilli. "I saved this for you, Sandro!"

"I thought you were being rather a pig," said Mondino's other daughter.

Mumbling her thanks, Alessandra didn't dare look at Otto again. She'd felt so hungry—but now that she found herself with food before her, she could hardly bring herself to eat. How would she hide her gender, at such close quarters, from this man who made her heart beat fast and her knees feel weak with a longing to be held in his arms?

"It pleases me greatly," said Otto, "to be rooming here with another student who shares my passion."

Maxie nearly fell over her own feet as she hastened to bring Sandro a goblet of water for the fit of coughing that had overtaken him.

"Be three times happy then, my boy!" Mondino said with a nod to Sandro and a hearty laugh. "All the students at this table are equally entranced with the subject of medicine."

Otto nodded first at his host and then at Bene. "We will all three of us be a merry band of scholars then, privileged to sit at your table, *Professore*."

Bene thought how poor a figure he cut among these

swells, with their rich clothes and fancy airs. He stole a look at Sandro, who was biting down on his rosy lips and largely ignoring the lovely piece of meat he'd just been given. This Otto, at least, looked and sounded like a proper man.

Bene vowed to find a way to win back his place, so lately usurped, as Mondino's protégé. Like every other man who was honored and admired, Sandro surely had a weakness that he kept hidden from the world. All Bene had to do was find it out and make it known.

They rode out early in the morning, the hawks hooded and held high, perched on the leather gauntlets worn by Mondino and his eldest son.

Otto stayed as close as he could to Sandro, who raced ahead with all the joy of being free and out in the countryside again. Alessandra had a good horse beneath her, and no one—save Otto—was paying much attention to her at all.

Sometimes, when riding, Alessandra was able to think in a way she couldn't when she was standing still. It was as if she were racing side by side with her own thoughts—and an insight or a new idea would slip inside her. The sweetness of understanding seemed to be all around her then, in the air itself.

When the horses stopped, she tried to gather that sweetness close to her and hold it tight.

They were in a clearing on a rise overlooking a pond.

"There!" said Mondino, spotting the flock of ducks on the surface of the water far below. He brought his hooded goshawk close to his face and whispered a word to her while she shifted from foot to foot and jingled the silver bells attached to her leg. Using his teeth, Mondino untied the cord that held his bird's hood in place and hove his arm aloft. The unhooded hawk was suddenly airborne, flying toward the body of water below. "We'll have a duck for dinner tonight, eh, Dino?"

Gabardino, Mondino's eldest son, also launched his bird—a red falcon—its bells tinkling, into the sweet, clear air. "Two ducks, I should think, Father!"

Lodovico, Mondino's second son (who didn't yet have a hawk of his own) walked his horse up to Otto and Sandro. "There's a good place near here for wild onions. Come with me, you two?"

They rode another mile or so, following Lodovico's lead. Alessandra was suffering agonies of needing to urinate, and riding more was making the situation that much worse. She was grateful when they found the patch of wild onions and got off their horses.

"God, but I have to pee!" said Lodovico, lifting his doublet and starting to push aside the fabric of his breeches.

Alessandra turned her face away, furiously pretending to occupy herself with her horse's bridle.

"Come, you two!" said Lodovico above the sound of the stream of his urine hitting the ground. "Is it possible that you don't have water to spend after all these hours of riding?"

Alessandra was afraid of wetting herself, so desperate was she to do just that. "I'm going to check the woods for mushrooms!"

"What a fine idea!" said the good-natured Lodovico, shaking himself off and doing up his clothes again. "I'll come with you!"

Otto dug him gently in the ribs. "I think our Sandro might have some solitary business to take care of in the woods," he said in a low tone of voice.

"Are you too proud to shit with your mates, Sandro? Come—I could go ca·ca myself, now that you mention it!" He moved off a bit, away from the onions, and made to squat down.

"I won't be long!" Alessandra called over her shoulder as she ran as fast as she could toward the safety of the trees.

What a bother it was to be a girl sometimes! She found a place behind a fallen tree, where she was sure she wouldn't be seen by anyone.

The relief was enormous. She thought how much a slave one was to the body and its needs.

She was just pulling up her breeches when she heard a male voice—the voice of a stranger and yet oddly familiar. He said her name—her male name, but with an obvious sense of irony. She gasped and scrambled to her feet, wondering just how much he'd seen.

It was Bene, standing to his full height with his arms crossed and a pugnacious look on his freckled face. "Sandro!" he repeated.

"What are you doing here?"

"Oh, I wasn't invited on the hunt, was I? Butchers'

boys don't go hunting, do they? Not with hawks, and not on horses."

"They told me you wanted to study this morning."

Bene snorted. "Yes, as it happens, I was studying anatomy this morning, and a curious difference between males and females, Sandro! What is your real name, anyway, you witch? And what gave you the notion that you could get away with this—abomination? Do you think the scholars of the University of Bologna will take it lightly, being mocked in this way?"

"Bene—"

"Don't come near me!"

Alessandra nonetheless took a step closer to him. "Bene, you of all people should understand!" She spoke in a whisper, as she would have spoken to a wild, enraged animal. "There was no other way for me to come here as a scholar. You yourself have no doubt had to contend with a great deal to lift yourself above the state you were born into."

"At least I was born a man!"

"It was your good fortune—not only to be born a man but to have the intellectual abilities that allow you to pursue an academic degree. I have the ability, Bene—it is only my gender that is wrong!"

"It is a sin to try to change it."

"I don't wish to change it! I only wish to study and learn." She came even closer. "Do you remember how that felt, when you were still a boy in your village—when you'd learned and read everything you could there?"

With a gesture that was still very much like that of a young boy, Bene put both his hands over his slightly protuberant ears. "It's not the same," he said, a little too loudly.

Alessandra looked at him, at a loss as to what to do next. Finally she said, "Are you going to tell the others?"

"I won't listen to you!"

There was only one thing left to do. Alessandra reached inside her doublet and brought out her knife.

And then she yanked at her chemise, cut the hem open, and pulled out her hunk of gold. She looked at the flecks of blue paint that still adhered to it—the last traces of the image of her mother painted by Old Fabio. "It's all I have," she said, "and I'll give half of it to you if you will keep my secret safe."

Bene grabbed at the gold and bit down on it—then inspected the marks he'd left on it with his teeth. It felt wonderfully hot and heavy in his hands.

"All of it," he said.

"But I'll have nothing to live on!"

"What's that to me? You'll have your life, won't you? It won't be worth two *soldi* if Bologna finds out your deception. You'll be burned at the stake!"

Someone was calling "Sandro!" in the distance.

"You can't leave me with nothing!"

"Watch me, then!"

There was the sound of footsteps through the leaves.

"There you are!" said Otto, all outlined in sunbeams. Then, "Bene! I thought you were studying. Did you come here on foot?" He looked from Bene to Alessandra. "Is everything all right here?"

Bene smiled. "Just fine," he said, slipping the hunk of gold into his pouch. "Isn't it, Sandro?"

"Yes," said Alessandra miserably.

"Well, then," said Otto. "We can all go back together. Sandro, why don't you ride with me and let Bene ride your horse? You're by far the lightest among us."

"I'll walk," said Alessandra.

"Don't be silly," said Otto. "Come on—Lodovico is waiting."

What was the proper way for a man to ride behind another man? Alessandra, who was used to holding on tight when she rode behind her brother, thought she'd better try to somehow stay on the horse without touching Otto at all. But then he pulled her up so that she was sitting in front of him. "It's safer this way," he said, so close to her that she could feel his warm breath on her face.

The ride was an agony of trying not to rub against Otto—fairly impossible, under the circumstances—and a weird sensation of pleasure when she did. She'd never experienced anything like it before: his chest pressed up against her back, her bottom brushing against his thighs. It was very much like having an itch and longing to scratch it—but this itch was not anyplace she could reach or even locate. The feeling was all over her and somehow underneath her skin. She tried to remember if Aristotle had written anything about it—an all-over itch engendered by two people coming into bodily contact with each other. But she couldn't recall ever having read of the phenomenon.

Her agony was compounded, of course, by the knowledge that Bene had just ruined her life. She watched him and noted, with a useless feeling of satisfaction, that he rode poorly. What ill luck that she had needed to relieve herself just then, with Bene lurking close by! He must have set out to trap her. Why else would he be up on the mountains instead of studying, as he said he was going to do?

She should never have shown him the gold! If she'd only told him about it, she could have cut off a large piece of it for herself. He'd never have known the difference. But, then, she reasoned, maybe he wouldn't have believed that she possessed such a treasure, if she'd only spoken of it. And then he surely would have told Otto, and everyone else, what he'd seen—and then she'd have been done for.

She only hoped that Bene, although only a butcher's son, would still prove himself to be a man of honor.

❖ ❖ ❖

They found the others by the water with hooded birds again, standing over their kill. Mondino was in a merry mood. "All right," he said. He tossed a dead duck to each of them. "Knives out. Let's see who can gut theirs fastest!"

Alessandra worked with all the urgency brought on by her dread—and a dawning, desperate hope that perhaps Mondino himself would find some way to employ her, in exchange for her room and board. She could go to him, as Sandro, and tell him that she'd had a sudden reversal of fortune—that she'd have to leave Bologna, return home, and give up her education if some financial remedy couldn't be found.

Or perhaps, she thought with some bitterness, she could simply give in to her family's wishes and marry whatever scurvy man her father had picked out for her. He was rich, after all. But what chance was there that he'd allow his wife to study medicine? If her father had refused her—her father, who loved her more than anyone else in the world—how could she even dream of another man giving her greater license? She would be doomed to stay and serve this great landowner in one or more of his stupid castles, ordering his servants around and carrying his keys. He'd get her pregnant and then her life of learning—and maybe even her very life—would well and truly be done for.

Alessandra wielded her knife as she dressed the duck, without even thinking about it at all. She made a clean cut and pulled out the entrails and the crop, placing the heart and the liver in the jar Mondino had brought along. Her duck was ready well before the others, and very neatly done.

Mondino watched her as she rinsed her hands and her knife in the pond, but said nothing except to urge them all to hasten back down to the house and the kitchen fire before the meat began to spoil.

On the lecturer's chair, high above the corpse, Mondino looked very different and far more intimidating than the fatherly person who enjoyed himself with his family on the weekends. "The knowledge of the structure of the human body," he said in a voice that was also different, like the voice of God coming down from the heavens, "is the foundation upon which all rational medicine and surgery must be built."

His two assistants stood below, flanking the body—one to cut and the other to point as Mondino spoke. "Always start with the parts that are most corruptible." The prosector, knife in hand, made a swift, clean cut down the center of the abdomen, from top to bottom; then he made another cut laterally, from side to side. The students gathered round let out a collective gasp. Most of them had never seen the inner workings of a body before—and here were the entrails of a once-living man, exposed to their eyes.

The corpse was fairly fresh, and it was a nice, cold winter day. But corruption had begun already, and the smell of it was revolting.

Alessandra tried to hold back the liquids that began to rise from her own gullet. The last time she had seen this sight was when she was looking inside her mother's own corpse. Her eyes stung with tears—but she blinked them away. A couple of other students gagged and retched. But Alessandra mastered her nausea and watched, fascinated, as the prosector lifted up the entrails to better show them.

Mondino read from his own book on anatomy,

quoting from Galen and at times interrupting himself to note points on which his own observations of the human body were at odds with the writings of the ancients. "We are only at the beginning of this new science of anatomy, and there remains a great deal to be discovered and ascertained."

There were murmurs of dissent among the other learned doctors in the assembly. The writings of the ancient Greeks, with glosses by the Arabs and Persians, comprised the entire basis for the art of medicine.

"For instance," Mondino carried on, undaunted, "Aristotle wrote of a three-chambered heart." The prosector, with some difficulty, cut out the heart and put it upon a cloth spread over the torso by his other assistant.

"But as you will see—" Mondino had to raise his voice to make it heard above the bits of conversation and argument and the inevitable jokes people always feel compelled to make in these situations. "The heart is divided into two chambers, not three." The prosector cut the thick septum dividing the heart, laying the two pieces side by side. The jokes stopped then, and the murmurs took on more of an admiring tone.

The smell was getting worse, though, and a couple of other students turned and retched into the containers that had been placed by a servant, for that purpose, around the courtyard.

Mondino continued. "I quote from our translation of Galen: 'The blood reaching the right side of the heart goes through invisible pores in the septum to the left side, where it mixes with air to create spirit and then is distributed to the rest of the body.'"

Invisible pores, Alessandra thought. The septum had seemed quite a bit thicker and tougher than the other tissues, judging from the way the prosector had to work at cutting it. She tried to squeeze to the front of the crowd, longing to take a closer look—but by the time she'd done the requisite work with her elbows, Mondino had already moved on.

"The head must always come next, and last, the extremities."

It was in the last part of the demonstration that the prosector cut himself—not just a little bit, but badly, so that he was bleeding too heavily to continue.

Corpses were hard to come by. "Blast!" Mondino said,

suddenly sounding like himself again. He looked to his second assistant, who only shook his head.

"You know I'm no good at cutting, *Magister*."

"*You!*" said Mondino. He was pointing at Alessandra.

"Me?" she mouthed silently.

"Yes, you—I've seen your skill with a knife. Step up—be swift! The body is decaying rapidly."

And so Alessandra Giliani became Mondino's prosector, before she was even properly admitted into the medical school—and just in time to earn her room and board. All agreed—and Mondino most readily of all—that she was by far the best prosector he'd ever had, a veritable genius with a knife, with a subtle, delicate touch he'd never seen before in any of his assistants.

The only person present at the lecture who was really unhappy about the turn events had taken—apart from the assistant who'd cut himself—was a big-boned, freckled youth from Lombardia, newly rich and as torn up as the corpse itself with jealousy.

Alessandra could not live as freely as she had before. She was grateful she'd felt rich enough, upon her arrival at

Mondino's, to pay her room and board for six months in advance. It was unnerving nonetheless to feel that, at any time, Bene might choose to denounce her. But, after a few weeks of feeling anxious about the precariousness of her situation, Alessandra was caught up in the heady joy of being immersed in the very thick of the best learning environment in all of Europe for what she most wanted to study.

Even the knowledge that Otto—the one man to whom she'd ever truly felt drawn in a romantic way—lived just on the other side of a wall from her, ate at the same table with her, and seemed to take every opportunity he could to study, sit, or walk by her side, receded into the background of all the other details of her daily life. She forgot for hours at a time that she was anyone other than Sandro, student *par excellence* and trusted assistant to Mondino de' Liuzzi. Alessandra Giliani, the girl from Persiceto, began to seem a distant memory—rather like Pierina, Dodo, Nic, and the entire family from the life she'd left behind.

Alessandra had a favorite spot in a little garden near the Piazza di Porta Ravegnana, nestled improbably between the rival towers of the Asinelli and the Garisenda. The garden was filled with flowers in summertime and had a mossy marble bench near a little pond, where water had been diverted from the canal across the square. The lock on the garden gate was broken. And although many people passed by the Two Towers every day, it seemed that no one thought of sitting in the garden, which was always empty, as if it somehow tended itself.

It was a perfect spot to sit and read when she'd rented part of a book: quiet and fresh and sheltered from the wind. Alessandra wondered if the nobles who lived in the towers ever looked down and saw her there—for she would have been visible from high above. But if they did, they never lodged an objection to the slender youth who sat and read and wrote and thought, there in that little patch of Nature in the very heart of the city with its two hundred towers that rose like a forest of trees.

One day when Alessandra raised her eyes from the text she was reading, she saw a partially made spider's web backlit by the morning sun. Every strand was visible and shone as if made of the finest threads of gold. The spider itself was small but delineated—because of the lighting—

more clearly than she had ever seen a spider before. She watched as its silvery legs spun round and round in the bright light, as if each leg were in itself a separate living creature. It was indeed spinning its web: She'd never fully understood the significance of the phrase before. And she was dumbfounded by the intricate cleverness of it, this work that was far more skillful than that of any human weaver.

And yet it was only a spider—the very same kind she often killed without remorse, thinking only that it was far better to kill the spider than to be bitten by it while she was sleeping. This worker of miracles. This master artisan. This minuscule, animated jewel-like part of God's creation.

Alessandra worked hard to keep her changing body well hidden from everyone, but her growing breasts were more and more difficult to hide beneath the length of cloth she wound around her chest, binding it as tight as she could without constricting her breathing. It was especially irk-some in the summertime and the harvest season, when it made her sweat. Sometimes, while she wrapped the cloth around herself, she thought how like a shroud it was, as if she were being prepared for burial while still alive.

She bought great quantities of cloth every month, not only to bind her breasts but also to catch the bloody flux that came out her opening every time the moon was full.

It seemed to be a rule of life, Alessandra noticed, that people saw only what they expected to see. The magicians and conjurors who performed every day in the Piazza Maggiore depended on it—as did perhaps some of the more publicly renowned miracle workers and saints (although Alessandra would never have voiced this opinion aloud).

She might have wondered what truths she herself was failing to see because of the tyranny of her own expectations—but she could not see these in herself any more than the spinning spider could see the process of its weaving.

Bene certainly scowled at her even more than usual. But it seemed that the gold had sufficed to buy his silence. From the day of his windfall and their return from Barbiano, he took to eating his meals away from home. He didn't greet her if they passed each other in the city, turning away as if he failed to see her. After a while, Alessandra didn't think much about Bene at all.

She was very much taken up with her studies. Frustrated with the leaden translations of the ancient masters, she worked side by side with Otto to copy out the truest and most accurate renderings among the different versions they found. She was always buying candles and working by their light in her little room, far into the night.

Otto was showing himself to be a rival for Emilia in his tender care of Alessandra. He often brought her lovely things to eat from his favorite taverns—pots of bubbling stew and delicious pasta, delicately flavored broth and loaves of bread to keep her strong and well, despite all the meals she managed to miss through staying late after lectures and engaging in learned disputations.

She thought how lucky she was to have such a friend. More than once she caught Otto looking at her in such an ardent way that, in time, she came to be convinced that he had fallen in love with Sandro.

The thought of this left her strangely confused. She

would not have guessed him to be one of those men who prefer the love of their own gender—but how did one tell, really? The ancients seemed to have taken such love in stride, especially when it was between an older man and a younger one. Beauty was beauty, after all, no matter whether the possessor of it was male or female.

The Church, of course, took quite a different view. Alessandra thought that if she ever were to love a man, she would want him to be just like Otto. She admired him in so many ways, finding in him not only a nobility of spirit but also a kindness that seemed quite remarkable. He was beautiful as well in face and body—strong and well made, yet graceful. It pained her, in these moments, to think that he might not—as a man who preferred men—be able to return her feelings, even if she could unmask herself to him.

And yet she knew that very unmasking might well mark the end of his affection for her!

When he sat with her, late into the night—as they parsed Latin together and she could feel the heat of him so close to her—her head swam with the frustration and unfairness of it. More than once she leaned so close that her lips nearly brushed his cheek. But every time she stopped herself, pushing herself up from the bench where they sat to go outside and gulp the cool night air—or simply telling Otto that she was too sleepy to study anymore.

Then she'd lie in her bed alone, thinking about him—there, just on the other side of the wall.

Things were going more beautifully for Alessandra at Mondino's than she ever could have hoped.

She treasured the atmosphere that supported her academic aspirations while also letting her drink at the well of family life. Everyone there, with the exception of Bene, treated Sandro with kindness and affection. Otto was especially generous, with his wealth as well as his time. He always included Sandro in the lavish dinners he arranged in town for the slightest reason—a saint's day or acing an examination. He shared books with Sandro, sat by him at lectures, talked about life and philosophy, and joked with him as men are wont to do when they spend a great deal of time together.

One Sunday afternoon, sitting side by side on a bank

overlooking a stream in Barbiano, Otto confided his fears about the marriage his father had arranged for him. Alessandra started—it was the first she'd heard anything about Otto's betrothal.

"I just don't know," he told Sandro, "whether it will suit me, living in such close proximity to someone I've never even met before. And not only a sheltered girl from the country, but one who has spent the last year in a silent convent. What sort of conversation can such a girl offer me?"

Sitting next to Alessandra, Otto couldn't see her eyes grow wide.

She told herself that there were thousands of girls destined for marriage who were shut away in silent convents to await their wedding day. It was true enough that her father did business with Otto's family. But she knew, from what she'd seen with her own eyes on her fifteenth name day, that her parents had promised her to a man who was, in Nicco's words, an "old git."

How she envied this girl who, when Otto was done with school, would sit by the fire with him at night, hear his confidences, and share his bed.

"Well," she said aloud, "I would guess that she'd be hungry for conversation, after all that silence!"

Otto laughed. "Would that she had even half the wit you do—although there's precious little chance of that!" He tossed a pebble into the stream below them, watching the ripples it made. "All the girls paraded before me by my parents have been particularly docile and dull."

"But you approved this one."

Otto shook his head, then leaned it back against Alessandra's shoulder. She could tell that he had bathed and washed his hair. He was the cleanest man she'd ever known. The smell and the proximity of him were intoxicating.

"I didn't approve her." He sighed. "I haven't even met her."

Alessandra barely dared to move. "And yet you're promised to her?"

"I put the matter into my father's hands. I was tired of the spectacle of all those disappointed girls—and anxious to be off to school again."

"But you . . ." Alessandra hesitated. "You like girls, don't you, Otto?"

Otto jumped up as suddenly as if he'd been stung by a bee. "Of course I do!" He and Alessandra looked at each other long and hard, and then Otto looked away. "Of course I do!"

He sat down beside her again, but with more distance between them.

Alessandra in her turn threw a pebble into the stream. "Do you think, Otto, that you could ever like—a book-ish girl?"

"I've never met one! But if I did . . ." He elbowed Alessandra gently in the ribs. "And if she were comely— well, then! Such a girl would have to run very fast to escape me!"

Alessandra leaped out of the way just in time to avoid being tackled by Otto. The leap turned into a game of tag between them, jumping back and forth across the stream until Alessandra's foot slipped and she landed up to her waist in the icy water. When Otto, laughing, extended his hand to help her out, she pulled him in after her. Half choking with laughter and each tripping over the other's limbs, they splashed and dunked each other until their clothes and hair were sodden. Otto pulled at

Alessandra's sleeve as she tried to make her escape—and the fabric of it ripped noisily.

"I'm sorry!" he said. "I'll buy you a new—" He stopped midphrase as the fabric fell away, exposing her naked shoulder . . . and the cloth wrapped tightly around her breasts.

He grabbed at her arms as if she were about to wash downstream. Alessandra, seeing what he saw, gave up on trying to cover herself again. She held herself straight and tall and looked up into Otto's eyes. "I am still myself," she said. "And I hope to God I am still your friend!"

He shook her then, so hard at first that she feared he was reacting much as Bene had—and her heart filled with dread. But then he was hugging her close to him, alternately patting her back and caressing her damp, curling hair. "Oh, I cannot tell you—" He was half laughing, half crying, and the effect was such that she couldn't tell what he was saying. "I thought—I wondered . . . ," he stammered, until finally she tilted her face upwards, grabbed his shoulders, and kissed him on the mouth.

"Sweet Otto!"

"Oh, my sweet—but who are you, my changeling?"

She kissed him again, and he kissed her back, this time with such tenderness that they both felt on fire although they were standing up to their ankles in the stream.

"Who would you have me be?" she asked him, pushing him far enough away so that they weren't kissing anymore, but close enough so that they might do so again at any moment.

Otto caressed her cheek in a way he hadn't dared—and hadn't wanted to—when he thought she was a boy. "I would have you be the girl my parents chose for me."

"And what is the name of that fortunate female?" she asked him, hardly daring to breathe.

He ran a hand through her chestnut curls and down her neck and over her naked shoulder, admiring its shape. "She is the daughter of the stationer Giliani of Persiceto. Her Christian name is Alessandra."

The love that Alessandra felt for her Papa in that moment—her wise, wonderful, brilliant Papa—lit her face like a sunrise. "You are betrothed to Alessandra Giliani?"

"I am, alas—but I will not marry her!"

"Oh, never say that, Otto!"

"But I love you!"

Alessandra kissed him again. "If you love me, you must promise to marry no one but Alessandra Giliani."

Otto looked at her, hope also dawning in his face and clearly doing battle there with doubt that such a thing—such a marvelous thing—could possibly be real. He began to speak but she hushed him, putting her hand over his mouth. "Promise me!"

He removed her hand, turned it over, and kissed her upturned palm. "I promise that I will marry no one but you!"

"That will have to do then." She stole another kiss, savoring the taste of him—and then broke away and ran back toward the house, covering her naked skin as best she could in Sandro's sodden clothes.

Thirteen

Mondino was about to leave Sandro alone with a windfall corpse that had just come to him from the hospital. They were by the river. It was early morning and the sky was bright but cold.

The body was that of a prostitute who died in child-birth. No one knew her—or, at least, no one would admit to knowing her. The hospital sold her body to Mondino to raise money for her newly orphaned child, who had been cut out of his mother when she died too soon to deliver him.

"I must change my clothes and make sure the runner has done his work," said Mondino. But then he saw the look on his young assistant's face. "Are you all right?"

Alessandra bit her lip and tried to look professional. "My mother, God rest her soul, died in just the same way when my little brother was delivered."

"A gruesome business! I would not myself be a woman for all the world."

"Magister . . ." Alessandra waylaid him before he left to spread the word in the medical school that he'd be doing a dissection. "When a woman is so exhausted from her labor that she's in danger of dying, couldn't the babe be cut out of her then, while both are still alive?"

"Only if the babe is a future king will a woman be ripped open before she's dead—because such a cut could only kill her."

"But if we knew more precisely where to cut, and where not to cut—wouldn't it be possible then?" Alessandra thought of a completely different childhood for herself, in which her mother had lived.

"It would take a miracle or black magic," said Mondino. "Certain midwives boast of having done it—but any man of science is wise to keep his distance from the likes of them." He clapped Alessandra on the back. "Carry on, Sandro! Get her ready and cover her up until I return with the hordes."

That night, after the dissection, Alessandra stayed up late in her room, writing in her notebook. She meant to go to bed. But then she woke, very stiff and cold, the remnants of a dream sticking to her like cobwebs.

There were two rivers, one bloodred and the other blue. There was an island in the center where the rivers crossed. The island was teeming with animal life, although Alessandra couldn't recognize any of the creatures there. But she could tell from the pulse of the place that it was indeed filled with living things—with life itself. The rivers were wide where the island parted them, but each one branched out in scores of tributaries, bloodred and blue, into streams of diminishing size with the smallest as fine as a spider's leg.

The oddest thing about these rivers was that they ran both ways, back and forth to the island, like a living tide.

She shook herself more fully awake—and then felt her way out of her room and into the kitchen to relight her candle. Maxie was sitting there, alone by the fire, doing a bit of sewing. She nearly pitched her little piece of embroidery into the flames when she jumped up to greet Alessandra.

"Sandro! You're still awake."

Alessandra's eyes were hurting. She mustered a smile for Maxie. "As are you! It's late and rather dark for needlework, isn't it?"

Maxie had hidden whatever she was working on behind her back. It seemed to be an embroidered pen-case. "I couldn't sleep—and I didn't want to wake my sister."

"You're a good girl."

"Do you think so?" Maxie's eyes were shining. "Papa told me that you're doing wonderfully well—he has great hopes for you!"

This was, of course, welcome news. Alessandra planned to petition the following year, if she could keep up the pace of her work, for admission to the medical school. Mondino's support would ensure her success—or at least Sandro's.

She sighed, thinking about the sweetness of Otto's kisses—and wondering if she would ever be able to be her true self in the world again.

In the dancing shadows from the fire, Maxie sat back down and patted the place on the bench next to her. "Come sit awhile! It must be cold in your room."

Alessandra looked down at her fingernails; they were blue, and she shivered. "It's quite cold there now. Do you know if Otto has returned from town yet?"

Maxie's expression changed. "Oh, Otto!" she said peevishly. "I suppose your room is less cold when he spends time there with you."

"It is much warmer and pleasanter here right now— believe me!" Alessandra plunked herself down on the bench and gave Maxie a friendly kiss on the cheek.

She realized too late the mistake she'd made. Maxie's breathing became rapid and shallow, her cheeks flushed, and her eyes were suddenly swimming in tears. "Sandro!" She breathed the name rather than spoke it. "My most beloved!" She threw herself at Alessandra, pressing her lips to Alessandra's lips, caressing her cheeks and shoving her eager little breasts against the binding cloth beneath

Alessandra's chemise.

Alessandra pushed the girl away from her like a swimmer pushing away from the shore.

Maxie began to cry. "I thought—"

Alessandra shook her head and impulsively took both of Maxie's pretty hands in hers. "It's altogether impossible. But you must not think it has anything to do with you!"

Maxie buried her face in her hands. "I am too thin!"

"Not a bit of it! You're quite perfect—any man would love you. But, I don't know how to say this to you, Maxie. . . ."

Mina came into the room then, her face lit by her candle. Alessandra thought she looked like an angel. "Then perhaps you should not say it."

Maxie ran to her. "Oh, Mamma!"

"Hush, child, and go to bed!" Mina kissed her elder daughter, gave her the candle, and sent her sniffling out the door.

Sitting down next to Alessandra on the bench in the firelight, Mina took Alessandra's cap off her head, tousled her curls, caressed her smooth cheek, and pulled the girl close to her. "Would you like to tell the truth to me?"

Alessandra's eyes welled up with tears. "I cannot!"

"Will you break poor Maxie's heart?"

Alessandra didn't want to ever have to leave the safety and comfort of this home and these arms. She felt so tired suddenly. She could feel the courage ebb out of her.

"My love of learning," she said, looking up into Mina's eyes, "has been the cause of a great deception."

"Cara mia," said Mina softly, using the feminine form of this endearment and—in those two small words— revealing that she knew the truth already.

Alessandra shifted her position so that her head was resting on Mina's shoulder. "Have you known for long?" she asked, barely able to muster the energy to speak. "Was it Bene who told you?"

"You told me yourself, my dear. Did you think I wouldn't find the soiled rags from your flux? Did it not worry you, being all alone and finding yourself bleeding?"

Alessandra sat up a little without leaving Mina's embrace. "I had read of it, and so it did not surprise me— although it made my insides ache, and still does." She sighed. "I am the elder girl, and my mother died before I could take notice of such things—and my nanny left before my flowering."

Mina was smiling down at her. "And what is your name, elder girl?"

Alessandra looked into Mina's eyes. They were filled with kind intention and a woman's wisdom such as she hadn't seen anywhere for a long time. She yearned to tell her name finally to another woman—and found that her heart was bursting with pride, because Mina would understand the enormity and the daring of what she'd done. "Alessandra," she murmured. And then, a little louder and more clearly, "Alessandra Giliani."

Mina took it in, pausing as if tasting something new. "It's a good name," she said, adding, "and one, I suspect, that will be long remembered."

"Do you think so?"

"Oh, yes," said Mina. "I am quite sure of it." She folded Alessandra in her arms again and held her tenderly.

As she allowed herself to relax into Mina's warm embrace, Alessandra experienced a floodtide of memories of her own mother. She thought how there are some things that cannot be learned in books or lectures but only in the experience of feeling them. In that sweet scent of a woman's flesh and the soft caress of firelight, she fell utterly—and quite to her own surprise—fast asleep.

Alessandra woke in her own bed without any memory of how she got there. When she ventured out to the kitchen, following the smell of fresh-baked bread, she was uncertain whether she would be greeted as herself or Sandro.

Maxie fled from the room as soon as she saw her. That still told her nothing. Mina was ladling polenta into bowls for Horabilli and her brothers. Otto wasn't there; nor was Bene. Mondino sat on the bench by the hearth, poring over a manuscript and writing notes on it. He looked up at Alessandra. "Good morning, Sandro," he said to her with his usual air of distraction. Mina met her eyes and smiled.

Her secret—and her safety—rested now with Bene, Otto, Maxie, and Mina—a veritable crowd of people who knew the truth about her. She wished that Bene was not in their number. He'd kept his promise so far—but she never ceased to fear that he would change his mind.

Alessandra dawdled in the kitchen that morning until she and Mina were alone. "Will Maxie forgive me?"

"Maxie will be inspired by you," said Mina, "as soon as she's had sufficient time to take it in. You've done her a service to teach her that romantic love is largely made of illusion."

"Is it?" Alessandra asked, unable to suppress a worried sigh.

Mina looked at her as if she knew exactly what Alessandra was thinking. "I said 'romantic love,' my dear—not true love."

"But how can one know," asked Alessandra, "one from the other?"

"True love," said Mina, "is something that reveals itself only with the passage of time."

Fourteen

Pierina was beside herself with excitement at the prospect of Alessandra's visit home. So much had changed since she'd been sent away to that wretched convent—and so much more was about to change as well.

Pierina had always felt the sting of being the younger girl and not nearly as smart as Alessandra. Well, no one in the parish was as smart as Alessandra, save their father. It was quite a trial being her sister—although (Pierina told herself) who would want to be as weirdly smart as Alessandra? Certainly not Pierina, who was generally acknowledged to be the prettier of the two, with her lovely blond hair and blue eyes.

She felt a twinge of guilt as she thought about the pleasant hours she'd passed in the company of her stepmother, joking and talking about Alessandra's freakishness.

Well, all would be well now, with this match their father had made for Alessandra with the first son of the great landowner of Lustrola. He sounded just perfect for her sister—equally enamored of books and study, and bent on getting a medical degree. How perfect it would be for Alessandra, to be a doctor's wife! Their father said that he was a fine and well-made young man, too.

He couldn't possibly be, Pierina was quite sure, as fine and well made a man as her Giorgio. But, still, she was glad that Alessandra wasn't going to be stuck with some wretched old man three times her age.

She truly wanted her sister to be happy. No matter what their stepmother said, Alessandra—however odd she was—was every bit as much entitled as anyone to the pleasures of this life, which, God knew, was larded enough in sorrow to make a saint of each of us.

Pierina couldn't wait to see her sister and show off her lovely new breasts, and to tell her she'd begun her flowering, too. Maybe she'd even beat Alessandra to the punch. Their stepmother said Pierina was young to have started, and she had to be especially careful, as she could be got with child because of it.

She told this to Giorgio sometimes when they kissed and kissed, early mornings in the workshop, when no one else was there. Pierina repeated her stepmother's warning—but both she and Giorgio knew it was a good thing they'd be marrying soon.

Alessandra found Mina in the garden, gathering vegetables for their dinner. "Oh, please!" she said breathlessly. "I need your help, dear Mina."

Mina put down her basket, and brushed the dirt off her hands. They bent their heads close together while Alessandra whispered her instructions.

When Otto asked about Sandro at dinner, and whether anyone knew where he was, Mina said that he was in his room and had asked not to be disturbed. Mina nonetheless brought a tray of food to Sandro's door, knocked softly, and was admitted inside.

After the midday rest, shortly after Sandro left the house, Mina waylaid Otto before he returned to town. "I was asked to give this to you." It was a piece of parchment, folded and sealed with wax. Otto waited until he was well away from the house before he broke the seal—and noted, with annoyance at himself, that his hands were trembling as he read it.

She whom you would marry waits for you in the walled garden beneath the Torre Asinelli.

Sandro

Alessandra had let her hair grow out again in Bologna, having discovered during her first days there that many of the scholars—at least those who were not in holy orders and had enough hair to be vain about it—wore their tresses long.

The dress that she'd brought with her from Persiceto no longer fit—so she'd borrowed a gown from Mina, who had a comely shape and lovely clothes. Alessandra covered as much as she could of her hair and the gown with

Sandro's winter cloak before leaving her room and heading for her secret little garden in the center of town.

The sun was low in the sky when she reached the gate that was missing its latch. The light was too low for reading, but perfect for the revelation she had in mind. She settled herself on the bench there, caught her breath, and waited for Otto.

"Surely your cloak is out of season," said Otto as he pushed the gate closed behind him. He looked at the eyes peeking out from beneath the hood of Sandro's cloak. They were golden with the light of the late-afternoon sun.

The hooded figure touched the bench. "Sit here!"

It took all of Otto's self-control to resist the urge to take her in his arms. He did as she commanded, and reveled in his knowledge of the lovely girl who was hidden there beneath the heavy clothes.

"Close your eyes, if you please!"

"Hmm—famous last words of the robber about to smash his victim over the head. . . ." Otto shut his eyes, wincing slightly.

Alessandra found just the right spot to place herself. She flung the cloak away from her and whispered a prayer. "You can look now," she said, shaking out her curls.

The late-afternoon sun was behind her. What Otto saw was Alessandra outlined in gold. Alessandra as he'd never seen her before—as no one had ever seen her before—in all the ripeness of her young womanhood, as sweet and perfect as a golden pear that falls into your hand when you hold it underneath. The stem breaks as if by itself, because the golden fruit has reached the apogee of its perfection.

There are moments, now and again, when time itself seems to stop. This was one such moment. Otto and Alessandra saw each other as Adam and Eve must have seen each other in the Garden of Eden.

He walked closer to her, but it felt to both of them as if the space between them was shrinking. He looked at her face and when he was close enough, held her by the upper arms. He thought what a fool he'd been to ever believe that this luscious girl was a boy. "*You* are truly Alessandra Giliani? I have not dreamt this moment? I will not wake?"

They both stole a glance at the discarded cloak, which looked a bit like a person who'd expired there and then among the weeds.

"We'd better check to see if you're dreaming," she said. "Aristotle would definitely want us to." She disengaged herself and pinched his hand, hard enough to make him cry out, although he was laughing as he did so. "Have you woken up?" she asked him.

"Not yet," he answered, shaking his head. "There's another test, though, highly recommended by Aristotle." Leaning close, he softly kissed her neck and then her lips.

"I never ran across that work before in my father's library," she murmured, cognizant of the sudden change in her voice, which somehow seemed liquid now, as if the very words melted as they touched the air. She leaned in with her face tilted upward and found the kiss again.

Unlike the kisses that had come before, this one lasted a very long time. Alessandra and Otto both were dizzy and short of breath when they pushed a little away from each other—but only enough to be able to gaze at each other again.

"Marry me!" Otto's voice had a huskiness she'd never

heard in it before. He said the words again: "Marry me, Alessandra!"

"I don't know," she whispered, his ear just next to her mouth. "I will not give up my studies. I will not let you—or anyone else—make me do so."

"I would not want you to!" he said, holding both her hands against his chest. "It would be like clipping the wings of a falcon."

"Ah, but falcons are dangerous birds!" She pressed her hands against him. "Your heart is beating fast, Otto."

"And yours?" He slipped his hand under her chemise.

"Oh!" she gasped. And then, with a medical student's interest, she noticed the bulge in his breeches. "Oh!" she said again.

"Darling girl," he laughed, "my blood is rioting. And we must marry—we must! Without delay."

They kissed again—a long, lingering, deliriously happy kiss.

Alessandra pushed him away and gulped the air. He took her hands in both of his, and brought them to his lips.

There was the oddest sensation in her hands then—

and she looked at them, as if expecting to see them glow-ing with heavenly light. She remembered that day—so long ago now—that she had looked at her hands, just so, in her father's workshop. They were the hands of a woman now—and she knew their skill.

"As soon as we can, then, sweet Otto, we must look for a way to live together as man and wife."

Nicco ran across his father in the stables, just as Carlo was about to climb onto his horse.

"Good timing, Nic! Give your old man a leg up, will you?"

Nicco laced his fingers together and let Carlo step into the sling they made. "May I ride out with you, sir?" he said, wiping his hands on his breeches.

Carlo took a moment to consider this. And then he shook his head. "Stay here and look out for our women."

"Are you going away again?" Nicco eyed the well-packed saddlebags. "We might want to consult the planets first."

"I have already—and found no injunction against travel."

Nicco eyed his father warily. "You'll see Alessandra?"

"Not likely!" Carlo laughed. "I'm off to Bologna to meet her bridegroom."

"Wasn't that the sound of thunder?"

"Nonsense! You're as nervous as an old lady."

"Well, then," said Nicco, calculating how far he'd have to let his father get before he could overtake him undetected on the road. "*Buon viaggio*, Father! Make sure this Lustrolano has all the parts he needs to give me a nephew!"

"I will—and I'm going to do my best to see he hurries up about it." He lowered his voice. "Pierina is giving me cause to think we'd better have this wedding soon."

"Good Lord—Godspeed, then!"

"Godspeed, my son! With luck, I'll clinch a wedding date before we meet again."

"If only it were possible!" Nicco said under his breath as his father disappeared in a wake of dust. Then he ran toward the house to pack himself a few supplies, scattering the chickens in his path.

Fifteen

Alessandra, still wearing Mina's dress but with the cloak thrown over her arm, walked through the twilight into the crooked alleys of the district where the midwives and witches of Bologna were said to practice their arts.

She found herself on a street filled exclusively with women, apart from the urchins rushing about in their last games before heeding their mothers' calls to come indoors. The stars began to bloom in an inky sky of periwinkle blue.

She stopped at an apothecary's stall, noting that the

building looked a bit larger and better maintained than those on either side of it. Ducking inside, she saw jars and pots of herbs and tinctures lined up in neat rows on shelves behind the counter. A young girl sat on the floor, pounding some kind of root to a powder in a large mortar made of bronze. There was a fire burning in the grate, and the herbs hanging in dried bunches from the ceiling gave the place the scent of the wild hills Alessandra used to wander with Nicco.

The sign outside had the symbol of women healers along with the name of the proprietor.

Alessandra bowed to the woman who stood behind the counter sorting through a large pile of mushrooms. "Dame Edita, I presume?"

"I don't do abortions," the woman said without looking up from her sorting. "Go to Mistress Fulvia's, right at the first crossing and second under the portico."

"I'm in need of a room," said Alessandra, putting one of Otto's silver coins on the counter.

Dame Edita sighed, wiped her hands, and picked up the coin. Then she looked with narrowed eyes at Alessandra. "I have a room upstairs I've rented out from time to time." She looked at the unblemished young woman who stood before her. "It is few, the number of people who choose to live in this quarter if they don't have to. And you'd better know, miss, if you'll pardon me for saying so, that I will not allow prostitution in my house."

"I am a student in the medical school—and there you have it, *Signora*, my reason for wanting to stay here, where the men of Bologna know they are not welcome."

"Well, then—perhaps the room will suit you. It's simple but clean."

Alessandra smiled at her gratefully. "I'm sure it will suit me well—for both the refuge and the proximity to your craft. There is much that I would learn from the women healers of Bologna."

"That's the first time such a thing has been said to the likes of me by any scholar of the University."

"And none too soon," said Alessandra, accepting a glass of mead and sitting down. "I am no whore, *Signora*, but I am about to be married in secret—and my bridegroom will come to stay with me here sometimes. We agreed it would be the only place we could safely meet as man and wife, since in public I must go about in men's clothes—for my own safety, as I'm sure you understand."

The apothecary took all this in, nodding. "I will appreci-ate having someone here who can read. And I will be glad to teach you whatever I know. For far too long there has been no passageway between the two worlds of healing."

Nicco reached Mondino's long before his father. A very surprised Mina received him in the family's grand salon. "You're Sandro's brother?" she asked this tall and broad-faced youth with blue eyes.

"I am, *Signora*—and it's most urgent that I speak with her. Him!"

Mina laid a hand on his arm. "She's safe—you needn't fear."

"You know?"

Mina nodded.

"Our father is on his way, for other purposes—and he doesn't know that Alessandra is here." He wiped the sweat from his eyes. "I must warn her!"

Mina said, "They'll be hard to find at this hour."

"They?"

"Your sister has become—most attached to another

boarder here, her fellow in the medical school."

"Oh, that's just terrific," said Nicco. "When Father has it in his mind to get her married straightaway." He looked at Mina. "You say 'attached.' As fellow to fellow?"

"I'm afraid their attachment is of a more . . . passionate nature."

Nicco held his head in his hands. "If Signore Agenio doesn't kill him, then our father will—or he'll kill Father and we'll all be orphaned."

"Signore Agenio?" Mina started laughing.

"I do not speak in jest, Madame!"

"I'm sure you don't, dear young sir. But I doubt Signore Agenio would kill himself—and he'd certainly not want to harm his future father-in-law!" She smiled kindly at Nicco. "And, anyway, Otto is a most gentle and genial young man."

"Holy Mother of God—excuse me, *Signora!* Is it possible . . . ?"

"It seems to be," said Mina, grabbing her cloak. "And I think we had better go find Sandro and tell him that his days are numbered."

❖   ❖   ❖

Arriving at the Porta San Felice, Carlo was surprised at how worn out he felt. Once through the gate, he stopped at a tavern in the parish where Otto Agenio was said to lodge, thinking to refresh himself while finding out how to get there.

The tavern was dark and shadowy, lit only by a single candle and the firelight. As his eyes adjusted to the dimness, Carlo made out a sight that both shocked and upset him: two young men, hidden in a corner together and locked lip to lip in a passionate embrace.

He winced and looked away. And to think his own daughter had begged him to let her come and live in this corrupt and sinful place! How right he'd been to refuse her.

"I'm looking," he said to the barman who poured his drink, "for a medical student named Otto Agenio, said to board at the home of Magister Mondino." He put a coin down on the counter. "Do you have a boy who could show me the way?"

"There is no need, governor," the barman said.

"Is Mondino's house so close by?"

"Not exceedingly close, but . . ." The barman began

to speak in an exaggeratedly loud voice. "But if some-one wanted to find—*Otto Agenio*—he wouldn't have far to go."

There was no one else in the tavern but Carlo, the barman, the two men besotted with each other, and a marmalade cat curled up and purring by the fire. The two men sat apart now, one trying madly to hide his face in the folds of his cloak.

Carlo looked back at the barman, who nodded. "Oh, Lord," he said, holding his head in his hand. And then, "I will not countenance it!" He drank down his drink in one toss and straightened his clothes. "Signore Agenio," he boomed, "you might well hang your head in shame before the man who was prepared to give you his precious daughter!"

But it was the other man, the taller one, who came toward him. He faced Carlo, then extended his hand to his lover, a slender man who seemed hardly older than a boy, as Carlo now saw when he raised his pretty face and spoke the word, "Papa!"

Carlo staggered backward, tripped on the cat, and nearly fell into the fire.

Alessandra ran straight into his arms. "Can you ever forgive me?"

Carlo pushed back her hood and held her face in both his hands, shaking his head in disbelief. Letting go, he looked at Otto, but no words would come—or none would emerge from the battle of emotions raging inside him.

And then he said, "I will deal with you later, Alessandra!" He turned to Otto. "Do you understand who this person is?"

Otto dropped to his knees before him. "I do indeed, sir—although I will admit that it took me rather a long time to see through your daughter's disguise. But I can assure you that I loved her in both guises, first as a friend and now"—he held out his hand to Alessandra, who knelt beside him—"as my wife."

Nicco and Mina burst into the tavern just in time to see the newlyweds kneeling at Carlo's feet. Alessandra's face broke into a great smile at the sight of her brother. She jumped up and ran toward him, and he spun her around as he used to do so long ago, when they were both children. Once Alessandra's feet were on the ground again, Nicco took

Otto's hands, and enveloped him in a warm embrace.

"We must have a feast," said Mina, looking on.

"We must have a wedding!" added Nicco.

Alessandra and Otto looked at each other. "We've already said our vows before a priest. But it would please me greatly, Papa, if we could have a wedding—a proper wedding, at home."

They waited until just after Easter, when Otto's family journeyed to Persiceto. Mondino's clan came, too, as well as several of Otto's friends from the University. Every one of the students asked where Sandro was—and none of them saw anything other than the brilliant and beautiful girl Otto's family had snagged for him. Alessandra thought, once again, how people see what they expect to see, even when something quite contrary to their expectations is right before their eyes.

At her own insistence, Alessandra wore her mother's wedding gown, which Emilia took great pains to refresh and shake out. Pierina was happy enough to wear the magnificent blue silk dress, which Alessandra arranged to have brought over from the convent; it arrived in Persiceto at more or less the same time as she did. Ursula was so taken up with all the preparations needed for the feast—and so focused on Pierina—that she didn't bother Alessandra with questions or complaints. The girl was marrying at last—and to Ursula, this was all that mattered.

There was food enough to feed family and friends, and a bevy of servants, students, and beggars besides, over the course of two full days. Lodovico played the lute, Giorgio and Pierina sang, and Carlo and Mondino both got so drunk that they danced the *tarantella*. Mina almost wet herself from laughing.

The festivities went on for three days. Nicco flirted with Maxie so ardently that Horabilli began to think she would be the only one of the daughters left unmarried. The innkeeper of Persiceto made plans to add a new room with his windfall, and the stone mason was happy in his turn to receive more work, as his wife was pregnant with a new baby. And Alessandra and Otto were as delighted as any newlyweds have ever been, in love with each other and, by extension, with the whole world.

Bene had been invited, but didn't come—which every-one agreed was a shame.

With Mina's help, the newlyweds rented a small house not far from Mondino's. They let it be known that Alessandra's cousin—none other than the famous Sandro—would be boarding with them. No one who wasn't in on Alessandra's secret thought it strange to see Otto and Sandro together. But a couple of people remarked, in passing, that they had yet to see Sandro with his pretty cousin from Persiceto.

Alessandra went one day to the quarter where the Jews lived. And there she watched a butcher kill a calf, slitting its throat and then hanging it upside down on a hook overhanging a bucket. She actually looked into the calf's still-living eye while the blood and the life drained out of it, and she thought about the difference between the moment when it was alive and the moment when it was dead. She remembered then her dream about the two rivers, but had no sense yet of its meaning.

She passed a stall that had books in it, some of them quite beautifully illuminated, although made of paper rather than parchment and all of them written in what she took to be Hebrew or Arabic. In one of these there was a simple drawing of a person showing the heart and the lungs and—painted in bloodred ink and blue—the veins and the arteries.

She asked the bookseller how much he wanted for it but he only laughed at her. She went home and discussed the matter with Otto. And then she came back with two gold coins and bought the book that so intrigued her. She wanted to pay the Jewish merchant to translate the words accompanying the drawing of the heart and lungs. But he protested that he could read very little Arabic, and only poetry. Nonetheless, she made him write down for her, in the Latin alphabet, the name of the man who authored the book. It was Ibn al-Nafis, who was born in Damascus, the bookseller told her—everyone knew of him in the Oriental world. He was a great scholar of law, as well as medicine and philosophy, and had been the personal physician to the Sultan.

Alessandra kept the book close by her bed, where she looked at it every night, trying to parse out what the pictures meant even though she couldn't make any sense of the words.

On the days when there weren't any lectures she

wanted to attend, she took to revisiting the witches' quarter. Dame Edita was happy enough to have Alessandra come along with her to gather the ingredients for her medicines. There were hundreds and hundreds of these, from acacia to zedoary, from Armenian bole to sea holly, roebuck rennet, pennywort, and honeysuckle. Slaked lime, lizard, and knotgrass. St. John's wort and serviceberry. Wood sage and the juice of wild cabbage.

Mondino himself was familiar with such matters, as his own grandfather had been an apothecary. But Dame Edita's knowledge dwarfed the compendium of *materia medica* that Mondino knew by heart.

Aware that Alessandra could read Latin—and more trusting of her now—Dame Edita pulled from her trunk an ancient, recipe-stained copy of *The Trotula*, a centuries-old manual for the medical treatment of women, including beauty remedies. The book had been treated as a sacred object by her mother and her mother's mother, even though none of them could read it. As Alessandra, by candlelight after business hours, translated the book into the vernacular, paragraph by paragraph, Dame Edita only nodded—and sometimes smiled. The knowledge had been passed down to her, almost word for word.

But Alessandra learned a great deal in this reading—and it struck her how odd it was that there seemed to be a parallel world of women's medicine, where women were in charge. And another world of Oriental medicine, if her book by Ibn al-Nafis was any indication of the depth of learning there in the faraway lands of the Levant. It made her grateful that she'd come to this place that was shunned by so many.

One day when she was visiting, hooded agents of the *Podestà* came down the alleyway, pounding at every door, looking for a midwife who was known to everyone there—and yet everyone there denied ever having heard of her. They left with their pikes and their hangman's noose.

"Any woman with healing powers," Dame Edita explained to Alessandra, who'd been frightened for her friend, "whether a witch or a future saint, causes their manhood to shrink, and calls out the killers among them."

Later, when the two had gone out beyond the city walls to look for meadow rue and mugwort, Dame Edita said to her, "Be wary, my dear, about showing the full extent of your true self to any men—because their sense of rightness in the world depends on their belief in themselves as the sex that is stronger and wiser, and far more worthy."

Alessandra usually listened very carefully and well to what Dame Edita told her. But sometimes—as on this day—she did not take to heart what she heard.

Otto was proof, after all, that not all men were this way. He was always there to help and encourage her. And Mondino himself, once he had gotten over the shock of her unmasking, seemed to have undergone a change in his attitude about women. He even suggested to his own daughters that they, too, might—in time, and if properly veiled—like to start attending lectures.

When Alessandra mentioned to Otto that she wanted a pig to use for a dissection, a fresh pig was delivered to their house that very day. Otto assisted as Alessandra cut it open, starting with the most corruptible parts, just as Mondino had taught her. She asked Otto to write down things as she observed them—and to make drawings as well.

Pigskin was harder to cut than human flesh—tougher, so that she had to score it four or five times with the knife. There was another, thinner skin underneath this one that nonetheless adhered to it. The two could be parted with her finger as she slid it back and forth between them. Something invisible had held the two layers of skin together—something that now was broken.

Cutting through and tearing the incision open wider with her two hands, Alessandra tried to sort out the complexity of what was inside. Everything was fit together like a puzzle, but in every dimension and subtly—just like the skin and underskin, it was all stuck together subtly until she pulled it apart.

She had to use a mallet and Otto's help to break the ribs and pull aside the breastbone. It was such a mess of organs and blood inside that it was hard to tell what went together and which things were different, one from the other. It seemed to her that there were clear threads holding it all together, almost like the substance a spider uses to spin its webs, except much stronger. There was so much stuffed inside! Once she'd pulled much of it outside the body, it was difficult to credit that it all had fit before.

What a shortage of space God had allowed inside a pig's body for all that it needed to function!

When she was covered in blood and still hadn't found what she was looking for, she asked their servant to cook the pig's flesh and sell the rest for sausages. She went to bathe and thought about the dream again and the drawing in her book; it still made no sense to her, and yet she felt as if some important meaning hovered just on the margins of thought, flitting around in her head like a small white moth.

The extravagant gift of twelve more pigs followed in as many months. Alessandra filled half a dozen notebooks with her small, neat writing, and the servant rejoiced at all the smoked pork in their larder.

Alessandra perfected first cutting the pig's throat and draining the blood out of it before doing the dissection, just as she'd seen the Jewish butcher do with other animals. It made things neater, and she could see more of the vessels where the blood had been. Each time she examined the heart, she looked for the pores that were supposed to allow the blood from the right chamber to flow into the left, where it would mix with air to create spirit, which could then be distributed throughout the body. Perhaps, she thought, the mechanism was different in pigs than it was in human beings. Pigs, after all, had no spirit.

She opened her next pig while it was still alive. Otto was there to take notes for her. Using one of Dame Edita's recipes, Alessandra concocted a potion to make the pig sleep. She cut through the two layers of skin and the fat, pulled these aside, and saw the matrix of tiny rivers of blood converging in the beating heart and leading to the bellows of the lungs. She knew then that she was close to her answer. She wiped the sweat from her brow and said to Otto, "I want a human body."

He raised his eyebrows but refrained from saying how difficult a thing it would be, and how dangerous.

It wasn't that Alessandra wanted to put anyone in harm's way. It's just that she was thinking single-mindedly of what she hoped to do. A body—a human body—was the next step.

Corpses for dissection were strictly regulated. Alessandra realized that Mondino would always be the first person notified if a corpse became available.

So Otto, not wanting to disappoint his bride, paid

some students to steal a fresh body for him from the graveyard. An orderly at the hospital sent word to him when the woman died. She was a fair-skinned stranger. No one knew her, and she was placed in a pauper's grave. And less than an hour later, the three cash-poor students dug her up again. They pulled her shroud aside far enough to see that it was the right corpse, and then delivered her, in dead of night, to the address they'd been given. It was a sketchy part of town, where even they—three strapping young men—were frightened to go after dark.

Otto had wisely thought it best that such a thing not take place in their own little home—and Dame Edita was as willing as ever to be of help. She genuinely liked Alessandra. And, without telling his wife, Otto had been keeping the apothecary well supplied in silver and gold.

The two cauldrons of ink, with wax mixed in, were bubbling over the fire: one made blue with powdered cakes of indigo, and the other bloodred from boiled and strained cochineal beetles.

When the students arrived with their gruesome cargo, Dame Edita's daughter gave Otto and Alessandra cloths steeped in lavender oil to put over their noses and mouths and block out the smell. They had a hundred candles burning, so that even though it was pitch-dark outside, they could see nearly as well as if it had been day.

Knowing that this woman was someone who had a past and a childhood and family, loves, struggles, hopes, and a story—although all unknown and faraway—made it a much different thing to contemplate dissecting her. This was no pig.

Alessandra looked at her own hands and then at the stiff, gray hands of the corpse and her bloodless lips, and she thought about how the human body was but a container. God filled it up when we were born, then emptied it out again when we died. This corpse was but the empty vessel, Alessandra told herself, for what had been the woman while she lived.

Still, it was difficult to make the first cut—far different, somehow, than when she served as prosector for Mondino. But she said a prayer and cut—and once inside she thought no more about anything but the wonders before her eyes.

Alessandra drained and sponged away as much fluid

as she could from in and around the heart. Then she cut a hole in the lowest point—the apex—of the right side. Using a hollow reed, she injected the blue-dyed wax—and then watched to trace its course.

Like the inky squirt of a squid she'd seen while Nicco and his friends fished in the canal, the blue wax appeared suddenly, spreading just beneath the surface of the lungs.

She and Otto exchanged a look of surprise. The thing was as clear as clear could be: From the right side of the heart, the blood traveled to the lungs. She felt her own heart pounding inside her chest and took a deep breath, trying to steady her hands. Then she cut into the bottom-most tip of the left side of the heart while Otto stood by, ready to inject the red-dyed wax.

Something felt odd about the tissues she'd cut. Otto held a candle closer for her. Pushing aside the dead flesh, Alessandra saw what looked like a tiny round doorway—definitely an anatomical structure. She gulped and inserted her own index finger through the hole and then moved it around, exploring. There was a hollow space instead of solid flesh, like an empty room.

She remembered the movement of the pig's heart—

how it contracted and expanded in the chest cavity, as if emptying out and filling again. An empty room—or a pump! She sewed the hole shut. And then, at her signal, she and Otto each injected a large dose of the red dye, more than the hollow room of the heart could hold. While Otto held the candle, she waited to be the world's first witness to the pathway of the blood, through the invisible pores in the septum, from the left to the right side of the heart.

But not one drop of bright red appeared on the right side of the gray flesh of the dead woman's heart. Contrary to everything Alessandra had been taught by Mondino and all she had read, the red-dyed wax they'd squirted in spread down from the left side of the heart out into the body.

The septum—just as it seemed to be—was impregnable! There were no pores in it, either visible or invisible: Alessandra's teachers had been wrong.

She sewed shut the valve at the top of the heart where the blue dye had traveled to the lungs—and then she cut the silk stitches she'd made to sew shut the other doorway. She and Otto both injected red dye into the right side of the heart and watched to see where it would go.

The redness began to dawn in the dead woman's lungs, just as understanding began to dawn inside Alessandra. Blood travels in a loop: from the heart to the lungs and back to the heart again.

She thought of Ibn al-Nafis's drawing again: the rivers of red, the rivers of blue. The blood, all exhausted, went from the heart to the lungs, where something happened that gave it life again. And then that blood—red in the drawing—was returned to the heart, from where it rushed out again, bringing its vital spirit to the rest of the body.

She'd seen it first in her dream: the branches of the bloodred river and the blue. The island—of course! The island was the heart. The bellows were the lungs.

Alessandra felt her own heart, still alive, pounding hard inside her chest. It was as if everything she had ever seen or learned had been leading to this one moment.

The cock crowed. Exhausted and near the point of collapse, she wondered briefly what the woman had died of.

During the night's labors, Alessandra had nicked her finger with the knife and another time with the needle—

but hardly felt it. She gazed with wonder in the guttering candlelight mixed with the murky light of early morning, how clear it all was now, mapped out in red wax and blue—anyone could see it. And soon everyone would see it!

She told Otto that she would rest then, but only for a couple of hours. She used the waxy blue ink to write a hasty note to Mondino, and then dispatched a messenger to him. She and Otto went up to her old room above the shop, and fell asleep in each other's arms.

Mondino—wildly curious—was more than happy to let Alessandra take his lecture time that morning. Alessandra had told him of her studies with Dame Edita in the witches' quarter. Mondino had even gone there once to meet the lady, although the place was not one he visited gladly. A man of his reputation, after all, had to be careful—very careful—about whom he associated with and where he was seen.

The students gathered, as they did when the weather allowed and there was a body involved, by the banks of the Reno, outside the gates of the city.

Rumor traveled fast, as it does in the student quarter: an unusually large and distinguished crowd had assembled. Word passed from man to man, each vying for the distinction of being the first to spread the news that a startling discovery was going to be announced—not by Mondino himself, but rather by his famous young assistant, Sandro.

Many more people gathered that day at the river than usually attended the lectures. There was to be a show, people said: a magic show of some kind. The people were bored and restless, as nothing exciting had happened for several weeks in Bologna—no public executions, no battles between the Guelfs and the Ghibellines. No riots, no lynchings, no royal processionals.

It was a beautiful winter day, and people were happy to pack some bread and cheese and wine sacks, and make the trek out of town to the designated place at the riverside.

When Sandro unveiled the body, the most learned members of the crowd—including Mondino—pressed to the front to see what all the fuss was about. And then the murmurings began. The pronouncements were of wonder and admiration. There in the bright, cold sunlight, for all to see, the secret pathways of the blood between the heart and the lungs were revealed as only God had seen them before, visible now in the same bright blue and scarlet dyes that stained Alessandra's fingers.

"Behold," she said in a lecturer's voice, "the beauty of God's work!" There were tears in her eyes. Alessandra stood there dressed as Sandro, even though God and a handful of others knew who she really was: a daughter of Eve. A woman. And a scholar. A sister to Ibn al-Nafis. A daughter of Mondino. A descendant of Galen, Aristotle, and Avicenna.

Otto could not get close enough through the crowd to embrace her. He heard nothing but words of wonder and praise for Sandro and also for his teacher, Magister Mondino. And then Otto saw someone walking up behind her—someone tall and red-haired and big-boned. Someone he hadn't seen for a while.

It was Bene. He grabbed Alessandra from behind. Otto tried to push through the crowd to get to her. But Bene had already torn her scholars' robe and the chemise she wore beneath it. Holding her from behind, he tore the clothes from her body until her breasts were exposed.

"This is Sandro!" he shouted. "This is your prodigy!"

Otto knocked people down in getting to her. But it was too late to do anything more than cover her with his cloak and punch Bene. He punched Bene hard and called him a bastard. And as Otto wrapped Alessandra in his arms, he noticed that her skin was burning hot, and her tear-filled eyes were feverish.

A new murmur had begun in the crowd, breaking out now and then in loud, angry rumbles of speech. Someone shouted, *"Stregheria!"*—witchcraft—and a score of others took up the cry. This august and international gathering of physicians, professors, and scholars was quickly converting itself into an angry mob on the shores of the Reno River. There were calls of "Death to the witch!" and "Burn her!"

Mondino's sons, and Mondino himself, joined in helping Otto shield Alessandra from the crowd of men clamoring for her blood. Between the four of them, they were able to bring her, unharmed, to Mondino's house, although by a circuitous route. By the time they got there, she was shaking with fever. "My notebooks!" she cried. "Otto, you must make sure they're safe!"

He sent word to Dame Edita to hide the notebooks where no one would find them.

Mondino and Mina put Alessandra in their very own bed. Otto sent his servant out for broth made from a rooster. Mondino himself made a poultice to cool the fever, and then the fever was replaced by chills.

An angry red rash appeared on the back of Alessandra's hand. Mondino bled her, but only a little because she was so weak. She ate a couple of spoonfuls of the broth. She slept, and when she woke during the night, she was delirious.

The rash traveled up her arm. At times she met Otto's eyes and recognition would come into them again—and then she slept.

Her arm turned the pink of passionflowers. Mina called the priest. Otto sent a messenger to Persiceto.

She spoke so faintly, only Otto could hear her.

"Aristotle . . . ," she said, then closed her eyes.

"Save your strength, my love!"

She pressed his hand and looked at him, and moistened

her lips. "Although I revere him, Aristotle was wrong about many things."

This, after twenty-four hours of fever and insensible raving. And yet her forehead was still burning. "The three-chambered heart," Otto said, his hopes rising. "The unvascularized brain." He desperately wanted to spare her the effort of speaking.

She shook her head, and he could see from the way she winced that her head was aching. He looked over his shoulder, intending to ask Mina for a fresh compress. But Alessandra, with surprising strength, pulled him closer. "He was wrong about the capacity of women."

He smiled at her, trying very hard not to cry. "Spectacularly so!"

"He said . . ." She paused, her lips parted, gathering strength. "He said, 'The courage of a man is shown in commanding, of a woman in obeying.' By that measure, Otto, I am a coward."

"Then by that measure, my darling, I am a woman— for I am ready to obey your every command."

She smiled, very faintly; then closed her eyes again, resting.

He changed the compress and took her two feet in his hands, rubbing them because they were cold, then kissing them because he loved her so much and feared she was dying.

She sighed and seemed to breathe more easily. Everyone around the bedside was praying. But as far as Otto was concerned, he and Alessandra were alone together.

She opened her eyes again and looked frightened until she saw him. "Otto!"

"I'm here." He touched her cheek with his.

And then he heard the words, so faint as to seem from another world: "I would not like to be forgotten."

There was a slick of tears then between their cheeks. "You will not be forgotten, Alessandra Giliani!"

Even fainter. "Promise me?"

I found Alessandra Giliani by accident, in the course of looking into the life and work of another female anatomist who lived in Bologna four hundred years later, in the eighteenth century. The little bit of biographical information I found about Alessandra—this daring teenager who dreamed of doing medical research at a time in history when women were burned at the stake with very little provocation—convinced me that a novel just had to be written about her short and marvelous life.

I spent several weeks in and around Bologna, exploring

the vast holdings of the beautiful archives and libraries there, housed in buildings that are themselves works of art. I slowly parsed academic articles written in Italian, pored over gorgeous illuminated manuscripts, crept around in crypts, and stared at paintings. In all of these, I was looking for the details that tell us what it was really like to live in the province of Emilia-Romagna in the early fourteenth century. What did it feel like to be a young girl then?

I knew that all the contemporaneous paintings of scenes from the Bible had fourteenth-century people posing for them: These were Alessandra's contemporaries, whose ways of reading, sitting, working, learning, loving, and sleeping could be winkled out from these images. A wooden baby walker, a cradle with its rockers arranged end to end rather than side to side, a person hauling water, lovers sequestered in a private room at a public bathhouse, the very plants and flowers were all pieces of the mosaic I started constructing.

The place itself—the quality of the light, the way the birds sang, and even the drift of plum blossoms wafting down on me as I walked off the path of a pilgrimage road—all of these seemed like dispatches to me from another dimension, where Alessandra still lived and wanted her story told.

Now, whether Alessandra Giliani really did live is somewhat of a point of academic controversy. I was unable to find a written record of her name in original documents preceding the eighteenth century. One librarian to whom I spoke speculated that Alessandra's accomplishments were so at odds with all that was considered proper that records of not only her but also her entire family may have been destroyed. At least one scholar of medical history feels that it was, in fact, a chronicler of Persiceto in the eighteenth century who made up the whole story.

A funerary urn containing Alessandra's mortal remains is supposed to have been placed in the wall of a particular church in Bologna—perhaps the church that stands today in the Campo di S. Pietro e Marcellino. That church was covered in scaffolding during the entire time I was there. I am still trying to find more precise information about whether and where this urn exists today (I recently ran across a source that claims it's in Florence!). The stone of the urn is said to be inscribed with the following words:

In quest'urna le ceneri di Alessandra Giliani, una giovane di Persiceto, abile nelle dimostrazioni anatomiche e discepola, eguagliata da pochi, di uno dei più famosi medici, Mondino de' Liuzzi, attendono la resurrezione. Essa visse 19 anni. Morì, consumata dal suo duro lavoro, il 26 marzo, anno di grazia 1326. Ottone Agenius Lustrulanus, con la sua perdita deprivato della sua parte migliore, suo eccellente compagno che ne meritò il meglio, eresse questa lapide.

"In this urn, awaiting the Resurrection, are the mortal remains of Alessandra Giliani, young woman of Persiceto, adept at anatomical demonstrations and unequalled disciple of the most famous doctor, Mondino de' Liuzzi. She died at the age of 19, consumed by her hard work, on the 26th of March, year of our Lord 1326. This plaque was put here by Ottone [Otto] Agenius Lustrulanus, deprived by her loss of his better half, his excellent companion who deserved the best."

After I returned home from Italy, I continued reading everything I could find about fourteenth-century medical education and practice, child rearing and early education, home life, gender roles, and the production of books. Alessandra and her family felt utterly real to me (even though all the members of her family are made up, including what to me is quite a logical guess that her father might have been a stationer, giving Alessandra wide access—so unusual for the time—to hundreds of books).

There are records referring to Mondino's second wife, Mina, and all their children, as well as to their country place in Barbiano. All the facts about Mondino—apart from his personal interactions with Alessandra—are based on research. I don't know for a fact that Alessandra boarded with him—although that, too, seemed logical, given the way things worked back then. Bene is made up. But it was a practice for parishes to sometimes raise money to send one of their best and brightest to medical school.

I've tried to give as realistic a picture as I could of how books were made and distributed in the late Middle Ages. The University of Bologna—the very oldest university in Europe—was an amazing place in the fourteenth century, perhaps more like the University of California at Berkeley in the 1960s than anything else. The students were in charge. They hired teachers and fired them. If a student challenged a professor and could prove himself right—well, then that student became the professor. It was a true meritocracy and also probably a pretty rough and tumble place.

The advent of the university—and the sudden need for books—was as much an information revolution as the rise of the internet has been in our own time.

I never thought that history would become one of my life's passions. I never even liked history when I was at school, apart from the context of literature, music, and art. But history has lately been revealed to me as the place where I live, where we all live, side by invisible side with others who—if we get quiet enough and listen carefully enough—will touch us and tell us their stories.

—*Barbara Quick*

I have so many wonderful people to thank for their help, support, and encouragement that I hardly know where to start—so I think I'll start at the beginning of the alphabet.

Alisha Niehaus, an exuberantly gifted editor at Dial Books for Young Readers, was the catalyst who made me dip into the well and find this story. It wouldn't have happened without her prodding—at least, not this year.

Caterina Belloni, the Italian journalist who helped me so much while I was writing *Vivaldi's Virgins*, morphed into a full-fledged dear friend (along with husband, Maurizio), letting me rest and recuperate *en famille* with their daughters Ernestina and Maddelena at their lovely house in Lodi, near Milano.

Decio Armanini, one of Italy's brilliant biomedical researchers who doubles as an oh-so-busy M.D., was my host and guide in the beautiful city of Padova, where he arranged for me to have a private tour of the anatomical theater there, and he and his wife, Isa—also a doctor—shared their insights and entertained me.

Felicia Eth is the literary agent I always hoped to find—fiercely loyal, bristling with literary sensibility, and a person whose judgment I trust unquestioningly.

Giacomo Nerozzi, professor and reference librarian at the Archiginnasio—one of Bologna's architectural gems—was unbelievably generous in seeking out obscure facts for me and then reviewing the final novel from the standpoint of someone with local expertise about the history and language of Emilia-Romagna. His emotional embrace of Alessandra's story was and is of inestimable value to me.

Gloria Serrazanetti, the gracious head librarian in Alessandra's birthplace, San Giovanni in Persiceto, was fully engaged with my project the moment I made her acquaintance. She found sources for me that I never would have found on my own, took great trouble in making them available to me, and shared her intuitions as well as her bibliographic expertise. Her assistant Daniele even drove me to the train station. I will never forget the kindness and help I was shown in Persiceto—and I hope a statue honoring the memory of Alessandra is erected there someday!

Grace Cavalieri, the prodigiously talented and charming poet and playwright, waved her magic wand and showed me that there really are fairy godmothers in this world. I am her devoted protégée.

HarperCollins Children's Books brought a wealth of talent, expertise, and enthusiasm to the production and launch of *A Golden Web*. I want to especially thank Laura Arnold, editor; Suzanne Daghlian, marketing director; Maggie Herold, production editor; Elyse Marshall, associate publicist; Joel Tippie, designer; and Hilary Zarycky, associate art director.

Jan Gurley, M.D., has provided this writer with untold riches. She gave me a crash course in the anatomy of the coronary-pulmonary circulatory system (sketched on a series of napkins in one of Berkeley's great Indian restaurants).

She helped me understand the physiology of what leads up to and follows administration of the Heimlich maneuver. And, best of all, she has allowed me to be honorary auntie to her two wildly talented teenage daughters—Emilia Gurley and Grace Linderholm, who were the novel's earliest readers and generously served as my consultants from first chapters to final draft. Owen Linderholm has expanded both my high-tech and culinary horizons.

John Quick once again held down the fort and looked after the interests of our beloved son while I was off doing my research. Joolian Quick, said son, never ceases to amaze me with his creative spirit, his musical talent, and the power of his smile to light up my world.

Liz and Federico Minoli not only gave me the key to the in-law apartment attached to their magnificent flat in Bologna but unlocked the social heart of the city for me as well. I am more grateful than I can say for the music, the opportunities to wear a pretty dress, and the respite from my labors provided by their friendship.

Liz Stonehill stepped forward with an unparalleled act of generosity when the wolf was at my door in 2007, allowing me to keep devoting my time and energy to Alessandra.

Manuela Teatini, a writer and journalist based in Bologna, first interviewed me and then entered fully into my quest. I am enormously grateful for her hospitality as well as her insistence on driving me to Persiceto, where I struck bibliographic gold.

Maria van Beuren, chatelaine of Toad Hall—a beautiful-beyond-belief, invitation-only writers' retreat in New Hampshire—gave me the warmest welcome and the most magically fun and restorative week of brilliance and hilarity I've ever had in my lifetime. No one knew it when we were born, but Maria is—and will be forever more—my beloved sister.

Roberto Condello's perfect small hotel at the southern edge of Bologna's historic center, the Hotel Porta San Mamolo, was the center of everything for me—friendship, camaraderie, the best cappuccino, and kindness above and beyond what any traveler can reasonably expect. I will always feel grateful to Roberto and the San Mamolo's beautiful manager, Irena Lorja, for treating me to their warmhearted hospitality.

Rosemary Brosnan, my brilliant, sweet, and slyly relentless editor at Harper, made this novel so much better than it would have been without her ministrations. She got the very best out of me—which is what a great editor does, is it not? Rosemary, you rock!

Wayne Roden, violist with the San Francisco Symphony, *vigneron*, Italophile, and—magically now—my fiancé, entered my life just on time to take his well-deserved place in these acknowledgments. I created Otto—and then Wayne came along to prove that fairy tales do come true.

You'll find a detailed glossary, including medieval and Latin terms, at www.agoldenweb.com.